Sawbones

Other books by Catherine Johnson

Blade and Bone
The Curious Tale of the Lady Caraboo

Sawbones

CATHERINE JOHNSON

WALKER
BOOKS

...cters, places and incidents are either the product of the author's imagination or, if real, used fictitiously. All statements, activities, stunts, descriptions, information and material of any other kind contained herein are included for entertainment purposes only and should not be relied on for accuracy or replicated as they may result in injury.

First published 2013 by Walker Books Ltd
87 Vauxhall Walk, London SE11 5HJ

4 6 8 10 9 7 5

Text © 2013 Catherine Johnson
Cover illustration © 2013 Royston Knipe

This book has been typeset in Adobe Caslon

Printed and bound by CPI Group (UK) Ltd, Croydon CR0 4YY

British Library Cataloguing in Publication Data:
a catalogue record for this book is available from the British Library

ISBN 978-1-4063-4057-0

www.walker.co.uk

MIX
Paper from
responsible sources
FSC® C013604

*Many thanks to my wonderful daughter, Harry,
who loved this from the start and helped the book along.
And to my son, Ad, for my first ever visit to the
Hunterian, where this story began.*

C.J.

The London Gazette Extraordinary

Sir Robert Ainslie, our Ambassador at Constantinople, has at length procured a mandate from the Sublime Porte – that is the Ottoman Empire – to ensure that trade routes between England and India are not to be impeded between Aleppo and Bussorah and the Gulf of Persia. Difficulties between the Ottoman and the Russian Empires have also been discussed, and our Ambassador agreed that it would be injurious to our interests if the influence of the Russian court were to overtake those of England. The Russians seek to undermine the Sultan at every turn, and move against him where they can.

This last week Sir Robert attended a most edifying performance at the Topkapi Palace in Constantinople: magicians of outstanding skill and legerdemain, Messrs. Falcon and Finch, performed for the court and worthies. Is it too much to hope that these men will soon return and perform for their own countrymen in the salons of London?

The news from France is unclear. Without venturing as yet to form any precipitate judgement on the late Revolution at Paris and its general consequences, we can begin to distinguish, better than at the first moment, its motives and character. The massacre of prisoners in August is but one sign of the unrestrained and unchecked instability in the city and serves as a warning to those who would upset the natural order in any society.

ST. JOHN'S
CLOTH WAREHOUSE,

Lisle St., St. Anne's Soho. The finest muslins from India, the finest linsey-woolsey, tuff-taffety, organdie and all manner of trimmings, findings and thread. The best stuff imported directly from the Low Countries.

NO CUSTOMER EVER UNSATISFIED OR UNFULFILLED.

The most complete range in London or the southern counties. Open Morning and Evening, every week, closed for luncheon.

Prologue

Mr Charles Finch closed his eyes and winced as the knife dug into his skin. He bit down hard on the handkerchief and tried to think of good things: his daughter, Loveday, entering the vanishing cabinet with a flourish; the crowd at the Alhambra, Paris, cheering, on their feet. The heat from the footlights, the smell of tallow and rouge. A crescendo of applause.

The sting of the knife seared into his reverie. He wanted to turn his head, to get up off the table, but the surgeon's boy held him down tight, his head wedged sideways. He heard the blade close to his ear, slicing his flesh, pulling it back. He bit down harder. He must think himself away from this, from here, but the smell of cumin and coriander from the market outside reminded him this was not Paris.

The surgeon swore. Charles Finch's Turkish was passing fair but the word was unknown to him. The tone, however, was universal. Perhaps he would bleed to death and Loveday would never see him again. He pictured her face – furious, outraged. Redder than her hair.

He would not die.

He opened his eyes. Through the window the warm autumn sun winked on the water of the Bosphorus. The surgeon wiped the blade on a cloth. A drop of red blood dropped heavily to the floor.

"I make a space for the rubies." The doctor's English was perfect. "There will be a man in London with the young sultan."

Charles Finch tried to nod.

"Do not move. It will be over soon. He will cut them out when you arrive. No one must know, Mr Finch. Not one living soul, not even the ambassador – not anyone save your man at the Ottoman Embassy."

"How will I—?"

"You will be contacted when the time is right." The doctor stepped back, scrutinizing his work. "Then the young sultan returns alive and in secret and the Empire stands strong." He paused. "You cannot fail. Too much is at stake."

There was a scraping. Metal on bone. Charles Finch gritted his teeth. The money would enable them to live in a decent house – not Paris, the revolution was far too dangerous, but in London, with a garden. Loveday would never want for anything.

He imagined telling her about this a year or two from now. The secret audience, the palace surgeon, the rubies carried under his skin. She would think he had made the whole lot of it up.

At the edge of his vision he saw the surgeon's boy unwrap the rubies, flashing brighter and deeper red than his own glistening blood. The surgeon saw him looking.

"Do not think of vanishing with the rubies, Mr Finch," he warned, his voice as cold as his knife. Charles Finch removed the cloth from his mouth.

"No, I—"

"The valide sultan may be acting alone but her influence extends far beyond the harem. You would do well to remember that." The surgeon selected a fine needle and threaded it as carefully as the best Savile Row tailor.

"I would never…"

"Good." The surgeon bent over him and looked him in the eye. "The valide sultan trusts you completely. She must have her reasons. You carry the fate of our empire with these, sir. I have heard that men with your colouring are delicate. I told Ali Pasha I would have preferred another, not a … a foreigner, perhaps, to act as courier." He paused again and smiled a thin, unpleasant smile. "Mr Finch, whatever you do, do not fall ill or die before you reach London."

"I assure you, I have no—" Charles Finch gave a sharp intake of breath as the needle pierced his skin and the surgeon pulled the thread taut. He felt his skin tighten, then the pain as the needle pierced and pulled a second time. Charles Finch closed his eyes again.

Chapter One

Surgeon's Operating Theatre
St Bartholomew's Hospital
Smithfield
London
31 October 1792

The room was packed. Students and interested observers all crammed onto the benches that were set out around the room, and behind them even more stood, squeezed into any available space. The air was thick with the smell of tobacco and damp wool – the rain outside was unforgiving.

On the table lay a boy – a few years younger than himself, Ezra thought – white with fear. His leg, a mangled twist of flesh all shades from dark blood red to livid scarlet speckled with bright white splintered bone was strapped hard into place. The leather fastenings dug into his skin above his knee, almost as tight as the tourniquet. Two porters were holding his arms, keeping his upper body still.

"The boy fell from a ladder?" Mr William McAdam, surgeon, tied on his leather apron.

The boy said nothing.

"Yes, sir," Ezra McAdam said.

Ezra was sixteen, and had been apprenticed to Mr William since he could remember. He had the man's surname, but that was simply because he had none of his own.

"He was sent up to fix the tiles – he's a roofer, that's his trade." The boy on the table nodded, mute with fear.

Ezra passed Mr McAdam the skin knife and the flesh knife. He laid out the bone saw, freshly sharpened, and the artery hook; the wool for laying over the stump and the bandages for wrapping it after.

The boy's lips moved soundlessly and a tear ran down the side of his cheek. Ezra could tell it was the Lord's Prayer, over and over again.

"Gentlemen!" William McAdam addressed the room, one knife in each hand. "Your watches! I guarantee the fastest amputation ever performed anywhere in the world!"

The boy whimpered. The surgeon smiled down at him: a kindly, paternal smile.

Ezra felt every single soul in the room hold his breath.

Inside his head, he began to count.

The knives flashed. The skin was peeled back, the flesh pared away. The boy was screaming and screaming.

"Saw." Mr McAdam stuck out a hand.

Twenty seconds, Ezra counted, that was good. Mr McAdam's skill was faultless.

Ezra passed his master the saw and took the knives, wiped them clean of blood and flesh. Then there was the sound of sawing, bone resisting metal. One minute.

The boy on the table was suddenly silent – his head lolled sideways, passed out with pain. Ezra hoped to

God he would regain consciousness eventually.

More sawing, the creak and brittle snap of a bone cut in two.

Two minutes.

The mangled, bloody leg fell with a soft thud into a basket on the floor.

The surgeon stood back, wiping blood on his apron as the crowd applauded. He consulted his watch. "Two minutes and five seconds, gentlemen!" The crowd was on its feet. "I think you'll find that unsurpassed! Ezra." He waved a hand towards the stump. "Tidy this up."

Ezra flapped the skin back over the stump and padded it with a generous amount of lamb's wool. While the tourniquet was still in place there wasn't an excess of blood. He bandaged tightly, swaddling the poor boy's leg as if it were a baby, firmly, tucking the ends in – all the while imagining a life with only one leg. At least it was a life. And Mr William McAdam was the best in the business: with luck there'd be no necrotizing flesh or gangrene.

Ezra cleaned and packed up the surgeon's instruments. Across the room Mr McAdam had done with glad-handing the crowd, directing the most eager to his anatomy lectures at his house on Great Windmill Street. "Every Tuesday and Thursday, the mysteries of the human body laid bare!"

Ezra smiled. His master was part showman, part genius. His Monday surgery at St Bartholomew's was famous, and his skills unequalled. Ezra felt the scar on the left side of his face, traced it from his temple to the edge of his jawbone. It was almost invisible now, a slender ridge of lighter coloured skin. Mr McAdam's stitches must have been so neat – and of course Ezra had been a child, just five years old, when the tumour had been removed.

Mr McAdam was talking with one of the hospital porters, a small man with the pale, sunlight-starved skin of one who spends his working life under moonlight. Ezra knew the man, a Mr Allen. His second home was the Fortune of War inn at Pye Corner, where the men who bought and sold dead bodies gathered. They called themselves resurrectionists, but on the street they were known as grave robbers, body snatchers or worse. Ezra looked down at the boy on the table again, brushed his hair from his face and felt for a pulse. He was still alive; Mr Allen hadn't come for him. But when the poor lad came round – and he would, Ezra was sure he would – he would have to find another occupation. Tilers and roofers needed all their limbs.

Suddenly he realized Mr Lashley was watching him, right at his shoulder. Mr Lashley worked principally at St Bartholomew's; he was a surgeon too, though not anywhere as good as Mr McAdam, and bitter for the knowledge of it.

"Not bad, not bad," Mr Lashley said. Ezra stood away so he could see how cleanly and neatly the thing was done. Mr Lashley looked him up and down, taking in his black curly hair and dark brown eyes. "I had no idea your kind could be so well trained. If you find yourself in want of a position, you might let me know."

As the man walked away, Ezra cursed under his breath. He would no more work for Lashley than cut off his own arm. Mr Lashley was a surgeon to give them all a bad name, he thought.

"Ezra. Lad." Mr McAdam waved him over and spoke quietly. "I will be dining at my club tonight. Take my tools back to Great Windmill Street and wait up. Mr Allen will be delivering. Be sure you let him in without waking the whole household."

Puzzled, Ezra leant closer to his master and kept his voice low. "But we already have one thing, for the lecture tomorrow."

"This is an extra. Worthwhile, Allen assures me. And although I'd agree with you if you said the man was a sewer rat, I have to remember that we are hogtied and dashed without him. Please make both cadavers ready for an early start."

"Yes, Mr McAdam." Ezra tried not to show his disappointment. Anna had shown interest in a play at the theatre in Covent Garden and, even though he knew her parents would disapprove, he'd thought of asking her.

Mr McAdam smiled. "I am sure Miss Anna St John will wait."

Ezra flushed. Were his feelings so transparent?

It was still raining. Ezra weaved through the crowd outside the hospital, south towards Newgate and down Ludgate Hill towards the Strand. Past the shoppers and news boys, past the knife grinders and the gin sellers, the milkmaids and the shoemakers and the street singers and the card sharps. Even in the heavy autumn rain the city didn't stop.

As he passed the church of St Clement Danes, squatting at the east end of the Strand, Ezra pulled his jacket closer and shifted the heavy bag of medical tools. The church bells rang for four, the shops were lighting their lamps. Perhaps there was still time to see Anna before he reached home – if only to convey his disappointment at not being able to see her this evening.

Ezra ran from shop awning to shop awning as far as the cloth warehouse on Lisle Street, where the St Johns lived and worked. It was busy; through the window Ezra could see Anna's older brother David serving a lady and her maid, rolling out yards of expensive Indian cotton. Ezra knew Anna's mother and brother did not approve of him – no, it was worse than that, David had called him the devil's imp and told Anna to avoid him. And who would blame them? An anatomist's boy was not a good prospect. And even if he became a surgeon, he would always be mulatto. Luckily Anna had her own mind – and as sharp and quick a mind as Ezra had ever encountered in a girl.

Ezra checked there were no blood spots or gobbets of flesh on his jacket or breeches, just in case. Then he slipped into Archer's Mews, which ran between the rears of the shops, and stopped at the back door to the St Johns' home. The door would not be locked but there was no sign of Anna or Betsey, their maid, who was infinitely better disposed towards him than the rest of the family.

Ezra looked up at the lights in the windows on the first floor. He could hear shouting, loud and in French, and although he didn't understand a word, he could tell something was up. He hoped their friendship was not the cause of the row this time. His heart cannoned in his chest.

He would leave a note for Anna with Betsey first thing in the morning and attempt to arrange a meeting.

By the time Ezra reached the McAdam house he was soaked through and almost covered in mud. His best woollen jacket with the dark embroidery, his linen shirt and his good Stepney leather shoes were all drenched. He shivered on the doorstep, looking up at the four-storey double-fronted house that was both his home and his workplace; had been for all the life he could remember.

"Ezra McAdam, don't you dare drip filthy mud on the hall runner!" Mrs Boscaven, the housekeeper, glared at him as he dashed past, up the stairs to Mr McAdam's office and museum on the first floor.

It was dark. Ezra lit a candle and the room came to life in the yellow glow of the flame. He shivered, the damp was almost in his bones. He took the candle and made his way past the endless glass jars containing eyeballs and organs, dissections of goats and foetuses and human hearts; past the wax models of livers and lungs and brains, the flayed and boiled clean skeleton of the tallest man who ever lived, through a door at the far end of the museum into his own small bedroom. He changed into some dry clothes and a fresh apron. There was plenty to do, and at least it would take his mind off Anna St John.

The body for tomorrow's lecture was already laid out downstairs on the large table in the anatomy room, a large, glass-ceilinged hall that had been built onto the side of the house. It had two doors, one that led off the hallway and another that gave onto Ham Yard at the back, for the students.

Ezra took a candle from the hallway and unlocked the connecting door. The sound of the rain on the glass-panelled roof was relentless and filled his ears. He put the candle down on the table next to the cadaver and raked the sawdust good and even, then hung the room liberally with bunches of dry rosemary and bay. Only then did he begin to unwrap the cadaver.

The body was swaddled in coarse sacking: the resurrectionists left all winding sheets and shrouds in the grave. Taking either would be theft, and the snatchers knew how to stay within the law as well as they could. A body, according to the law, was not property, and no one could be jailed for taking something that didn't belong to anyone.

Ezra slowly and carefully unwrapped the body. It was a strange life; he knew that was what others thought, that they judged him. People wanted cures but they didn't want to know how to come by them. But William McAdam was no ghoul. How did people imagine surgeons knew where to cut, how to cut and how far to cut? You couldn't have one without the other.

He could still remember the first dissection he had ever seen. He must have been seven or eight years old, and he had squeezed himself through the crowd of medical students to watch the master at work. He had steeled himself then, as he did, just a little, now. Ezra sighed and brushed the mud into a pile on the floor, out of the way.

For now, he left a corner of the sacking to cover the face. There was something about the face of a cadaver, Ezra thought. It was not like the lively, animated face of a living man; that look, that spark, was gone moments after death. There was nothing left of the person the body had once been. The humanity had gone. Ezra knew this was true, not just a tale he told himself to make his and Mr McAdam's work acceptable. But still he covered the face – not because he truly thought the eyes might suddenly snap open and reproach him, but because he wanted to show a little respect to the life this cadaver had once had. This face, or, more to the point, the soul behind the face, had smiled, had laughed, had maybe blown someone a kiss. He let it rest a little longer while he looked at the torso, the arms, the legs. They would have plenty to tell him.

Ezra McAdam could read a corpse as well as an Oxford scholar could read Ancient Greek. He sometimes thought he must have seen more dead men than spoken to live ones. Mr McAdam said there was a lot to be learnt just by looking, and that's always how he began. Look first, notes second, he always said. Ezra had notes for every cadaver that had come through McAdam's anatomy school for the past three years. The master said it was good to know as much as possible about every single specimen.

Ezra lifted the candle closer.

The cadavers were not often Negroes. In the flickering yellow light he – and it was a he – looked almost well, his skin a deep, dull brown. He couldn't have been dead very long at all. Ezra lifted the left leg. It had gone through the rigor mortis and was now loose and limber, so the body was at least two days old. The discoloration and the settling of the blood in the back of the limbs told the same tale. There were no signs of disease, no necrotizing or ulceration – and anyway, it was utterly and completely obvious how this one had met his Maker.

Ezra took out his notebook. In all his years assisting

with anatomizing he could count on one hand the number of gunshot wounds he had seen. And they tended to be drunken soldiers discharging their weapons for sport – or perhaps shooting into a crowd at a riot, missing their target but harming some innocent flower seller or crossing sweeper instead. It was always the poor, the foreigners, the refugees who suffered the most, Ezra thought. At least in death, all were at last equal.

This young man was healthy, or at least he had been at death. Taller than average – a soldier, then, gun happy and drunk?

Ezra lifted the cloth he had rested over the man's face.

"You will do us all a favour, sir, whoever you were," he said aloud. "We will know more, thanks to you."

The cadaver, of course, said nothing.

The face was clean shaven, with a good bone structure. Ezra lifted the eyelids; the eyes were clear and not bloodshot. He smelt the mouth – not a taint of gin or spirits – and his teeth were good and strong. His hands were a gentleman's hands, manicured, clean. Not a soldier, then, and not one of the St Giles' blackbirds, men who had been slaves and soldiers once, fighting for the British against the free colonials, but who now scraped a living on the streets. Ezra made a face, deep in thought. Perhaps this one had been the loser in a duel. But a Negro in a duel? With pistols? Surely it would have been common knowledge, sung by every news sheet singer from here to Stepney and back.

The wound was just below the man's left ribs. Ezra knew Mr McAdam would be upset if the lungs had been damaged. He lifted the candle and brought it closer to the wound. It was like a dark red flower, black and foul in the centre, the skin forming red, petal-like fronds around it.

He hoped to God this wasn't a gentleman, some sort of wealthy merchant. If he had been a man of quality, that could mean a world of trouble for Mr McAdam. No one was too bothered about the empty coffin of an ordinary Londoner – and in too many cases wives sold their husbands; fathers, their children – but a gentleman, and a Negro one at that ... someone might be looking for him.

Ezra looked back at the face. There were no scars or marks such as he'd seen on visiting African royalty in Whitehall once. The hair on this one was cropped close, almost a shave, and there was a slit in both ears, as if Mr Allen or one of his kind had been in a hurry and pulled the earrings out. A sailor, then? But no sailor had hands like this, so little used to rough work.

The man's arms were well muscled, so he could not have been a merchant or an ambassador who sat in a chair all day. On the inside of his left forearm there was a mark. A bruise? Ezra lifted the candle closer – no, a tattoo. It had a definite shape, a letter perhaps. If so, it was one Ezra couldn't decipher. Possibly Arabic, he thought. Maybe a sea captain, an independent trader?

Ezra fetched a bucket of water to wash the body down carefully, the way, he told himself, he would like to be washed if he and the cadaver happened to swap places.

There were no more clues, save a lighter band on several fingers where there must have been rings. He turned the body over, and he could see the wound went all the way through to the back. The candle fizzed and guttered, and the room went dark. Ezra sighed. There was a stub on the shelf by the door, so he lit that and propped the cadaver on its side. Now he could see that the bullet wound on the back must be the entry wound. Of course! The flesh pushed in, the skin forced downward…

Ezra laid the body on its back again. The wound on the front was where the shot had left the body; when he looked closer he could make out tiny fragments of white bone among the pulverized flesh. This could not be a duel. This man had been shot running away. One shot from close distance – there were no other wounds. Whoever shot this man had either been close or had a good aim. Ezra thought how much more information he could have gleaned if he'd been able to see the man's clothes.

The body's mouth had fallen open as he rolled it over, and he was about to close it when he realized something. Or rather, a lack of something. In death the tongue sometimes swelled, he often had to tuck it in. But this time there was no tongue. He looked again. This man, when he had been a man and not a cadaver, had had his tongue cut out, and the wound had healed completely. It had been cut out many years ago.

Here was a puzzle, Ezra thought. How could a man run a ship, give orders, buy and sell, without a tongue? It was possible; Ezra had seen folk with no speech talk with their hands. The tattoo pointed to the cadaver being a foreigner, but even that was not certain. Whoever he had been, Ezra reckoned, a man like this would be missed. He would have to tell Mr McAdam. The decision would be the master's.

Suddenly there was a three-beat knock on the yard

door that set the glass roof rattling, as if the rain had turned from water to rock. Ezra, deep in thought only a moment before, nearly jumped out of his skin and almost dropped the candle.

It was Mr Allen, and he was alone, which was odd. It usually took two of them to bring the thing in off the pony cart. But Allen already had a sack hefted over his shoulder.

"Tell Mr McAdam it'll be the usual plus a half, will you, lad."

Ezra nodded.

The sack was small. It must be a child.

Ezra sighed. He would have to harden his heart some more.

Chapter Two

Mr William McAdam's Anatomy School and
Museum of Curiosities
Great Windmill Street
Soho
London
November 1792

It was still dark when Ezra woke. He could hear the city waking up down below in the street, the iron-wheeled carts trundling towards Piccadilly or the Haymarket, Mrs Perino's chickens cackling across the street. The church bells of St Anne's called the hour and were answered by those at St James's and, in a duller echo, by St Martin-in-the-Fields'. Ezra dressed quickly; there was much to do and he wanted to get a letter to Anna before Mr McAdam's students turned up for the lecture.

He dashed off the note by candlelight at his writing desk under the window. He told Anna that he could see her at lunchtime; they could meet in the porch at St Anne's if it was very cold. He sealed it with a bit of wax and pulled on his jacket as he made his way downstairs. Then he was out of the back door, past Mrs Boscaven arguing with the milkmaid, and back to Lisle Street. The whole city was sparkling with frost, everything glittered and shone and Ezra had to watch his step, as the cobbles and the new stone paving sets were treacherous.

The newspaper boys were shouting about wars in far-off places, Sweden and Russia and Turkey, and about the king of France, who in the midst of the revolution had tried, and failed, to escape his own country. Ezra bought a copy of *The Times* for Mr McAdam and tucked it under his arm.

The shutters were up on the cloth warehouse, and the curtains were drawn upstairs. He knew the family would not be up yet, but Betsey would have cleaned the grates and laid the fires and would now be hard at work in the kitchen at the back of the house. Ezra slipped into Archer's Mews and, seeing the candle lit, tapped on the kitchen window.

Betsey's surprised face popped up on the other side of the glass, but when she saw who it was she shook her head, frowning, and gestured for him to leave.

"Betsey, please," Ezra whispered urgently – she couldn't hear him, he knew, but he dared not raise his voice. Betsey didn't look convinced. "Please," Ezra mouthed again.

Then he heard the bolts being drawn back, and Betsey ushered him in. She looked disapproving, but there was something soft in her expression.

To Ezra's surprise Anna was there, sitting on a bench in the middle of the kitchen. When she saw Ezra she tried quickly to draw herself together and seem her normal, poised self, but Ezra could tell that she'd been crying. What was she doing awake so early?

"Five minutes," Betsey was saying. "Five minutes is all I'll give the two of you, and when I come back he had best be on his way." She turned to Ezra. "If Mr David finds you he'll skin you quicker than ever your Mr McAdam could!" And she bustled from the kitchen, leaving Ezra and Anna alone.

"Anna, what is it?"

"Oh, Ezra," she said. "David is to be married!" Ezra shook his head. He didn't understand. Her brother to be married – surely that would be good news? But Anna looked away, her brow furrowed. "He is getting married and we are going away, to Holland."

"Holland!" Ezra stared at her. Was this what the argument had been about, last night? "But your shop—"

"Mother will stay," said Anna, with a hint of bitterness, though she kept her voice calm. "But she is sending me with David, to the Hague, to live with my cousins." Her hands bunched in the cloth of her dress. She looked tired – perhaps she had not slept at all.

Ezra felt a knot of pain in his chest. He would have said it was his heart breaking, but he knew, from the number of hearts he had seen in a variety of sections and cross-sections, that hearts were only pumps made flesh, and could not make you feel like this. "But surely, if you wanted to, you could stay?"

"Do you think I don't want to?" Anna cried. "Do you think I wouldn't sooner stay here? I love London." And perhaps he was only fooling himself, but the way she looked at him then allowed him to hope it was not only London she would miss. "But Mother insists. She says my prospects will be better in Holland."

Ezra had to look away. He knew what that meant. In Holland, Mrs St John was no doubt hoping, Anna would spend her time in the company of young men more suitable than a mulatto surgeon's boy.

"When?" he asked, hopelessly.

"A week," Anna whispered.

There was the sound of a door slamming somewhere up in the St John house, and Anna jumped.

"You have to go," she said, and she looked close to tears again but Ezra knew she wouldn't cry in front of him.

Ezra wanted to weep too.

He walked slowly home to Great Windmill Street. He would have to imagine a future without his oldest friend, Anna St John. She would be living a new life in Holland. Without him. He swallowed. He would have to immerse himself in work as throroughly as possible.

Back at the house, Mrs Boscaven had breakfast on in the kitchen. Though he was chilled to the bone, Ezra couldn't stomach the porridge she had made, and sipped his coffee with the maid, Ellen, and Mr McAdam's valet and footman, Henry Toms.

"I reckon," Toms said, grinning as he helped himself to Ezra's portion of porridge, "as you've just found out about the St John girl pushing off back to where she comes from." Toms was only a year or so older than Ezra but liked to think it made all the difference as far as knowledge of worldly matters went.

Mrs Boscaven tutted. Ezra gritted his teeth; it was all he could do to keep his face from betraying his feelings.

Toms went on, "Going away with her brother, I heard.

Didn't want no brown babies! 'Specially not ones whose daddy might have been in a freak show!" He tipped his head on one side and held a breakfast roll up as if it were attached to the side of his face like a tumour, and laughed. "Or worse, someone who's only worth tuppence and should be sold back to the West Indies where he came from!"

Ezra pushed his chair back and got up, fists ready. He was going to punch the idiot into next week. Mrs Boscaven put a hand on his shoulder.

"Don't you dare talk that way, Henry Toms!" she said sharply. "Or I'll make sure the master knows what happens to the ends of his candles, and his soap. And that pair of breeches you swore blind went missing."

Toms looked shifty. Ezra didn't sit back down. He took his coffee and left.

It was light in the anatomy room. Ezra had covered both cadavers with a sheet the night before; they lay side by side on the dark, stained table. Ezra sipped his coffee. He was not a slave and he was not a freak. He pushed Toms' words away – he had work to do. Outside he could hear the first of the students queuing up in the cold. He reminded himself he had to see Mr McAdam before the lecture began, tell him about the tongueless man, the gunshot and the tattoo.

Ezra looked up through the glass roof to the iron-grey sky. He sighed and wished he were somewhere else.

"Ah, Ezra, here all ready!" Mr McAdam swept into the room. "Open the doors and let the poor frozen truth seekers in, lad."

Ezra put down his coffee cup and tied on his apron. "Sir, please. There's something I need to show you first."

"The child? Has putrefaction set in?" The surgeon took a deep breath in. "Aah! You've made good with the rosemary. It smells more like a herb garden than an anatomizing room."

"Thank you, sir. No, sir. It's the man." Ezra lifted up the sheet. "It's a shot wound. And not a duel with pistols. He's a Negro, and the word of such a fight would have been all over the city."

"You're right, lad. Well spotted. What else?" Mr McAdam took his glasses out of his waistcoat pocket and put them on.

"His hands, sir – a gentleman's hands. He must be wealthy, sir. And, by the look of things, shot in the back."

Mr McAdam raised an eyebrow.

"One more thing, sir," Ezra said. "He's had his tongue cut away."

"Recently? In death?"

"No, a long time ago. See? Oh, and sir, you see this mark, on his forearm, I couldn't…"

McAdam leant closer and picked up the lifeless limb. "Arabic. Could be Persian. Makes sense. The rulers of those houses often cut the tongues of their servants."

"But his hands, sir…"

"There is more than one kind of work, Ezra."

Mr McAdam said nothing for a long time. He looked again in the man's mouth, then at where the earrings had been pulled out of his ears, and at the gunshot wound. Finally he looked up. They could hear the crowd waiting on the other side of the door, shuffling and stamping their feet to keep warm in the cold.

"This is an odd fish and no mistake," he said at last. "Belonged to someone important, no doubt."

"Belonged? He was a slave?"

"I would think so. We must hope his master doesn't miss him. I could make enquiries at the Ottoman Embassy. Met a fellow at a surgeon's dinner, can't for the life of me remember his name. Ali? Aziz? Worked as a surgeon for the sultan, apparently. Perhaps our man here is one of theirs. How's the child?"

"Nothing unusual there, sir," Ezra said. "Drowned, I reckon. Five, six days ago. Some putrefaction in the eyes. The skin on the hands and fingers is beginning to slip. Signs of the rickets. If he'd not drowned I don't think this one would've been long for this world."

McAdam nodded. "Good, good." He frowned thoughtfully. "If anyone asks, we'll say the man died on a boat come in from the West Indies. Ezra, fetch the bone saw. We'll open him up before they come in and the students will be too busy swooning at their first sight of a man's heart *in situ* to see the gunshot or the tattoo."

"As you wish, sir."

"Oh, and buck up, lad. Your face is a mask of sorrow." Mr McAdam began to saw through the man's sternum. He spoke up to be heard above the noise of metal on bone. "Mrs Boscaven has told all, and I assure you, I too know the pangs of first love. The trick, my boy, is to kill your feelings, just as we do every day in here. Dispatch those tender emotions just as swiftly and cleanly as one would a sick horse. Brooding is neither healthy nor productive." Mr McAdam smiled. "Unless, perhaps, one is a poet!"

"No, sir," Ezra said, taking the saw and wiping it clean. It seemed every soul in the parish knew his business! Why, he would not have been surprised if the man on the table had piped up to offer advice, even with only half a tongue.

The students had gone. Ezra was sewing up the cadavers, ready for Mr Allen and his company to come and dispose of them once darkness fell. He had cleaned the sawdust and removed the bucket of vomit that one would-be surgeon had filled on discovering the contents of the adult cadaver's stomach. The smell of partially digested food, which Mr McAdam had eagerly shown his students, had obviously proved too much.

Ezra, having seen the insides of man and boy many times over, had spent the lecture trying hard to think about anything other than Anna. Holland was not so far away, he told himself. After all, this man on the table had travelled twice as far at least. As, of course, had he, from Jamaica to England, a long time ago.

She would write. She *would* write. He sighed and looked down at the tall man on the table, sewn up smartly; imposing even in death, but in life, slave, subject to another's orders with no independence of thought or action. Ezra felt powerless. He was no better, he reasoned, than a kind of slave. He had no money of his own, made no decisions. How would he ever travel to see her?

Ezra finished his work and covered the cadaver before moving on to the child. Of course he didn't *have* to sew them up: the paupers these two corpses would be sharing graves with would not care whether or not the contents of their winding sheets were intact. No, but it was good practice. Ezra wanted his stitches to be as good as his master's. Small, neat, perfect.

"Aha, Ezra. Still hard at work." Mr McAdam looked over his stitches. "You have a good hand, lad. A good hand. You will make a fine surgeon."

"Thank you, sir." Ezra looked up; the master was smiling. Perhaps there was a way around his current problem. "Sir, if you please, I would ask you a question. If you have a moment."

"Of course," Mr McAdam said. "Ask away."

Ezra put down his needle. He took a deep breath. "I was thinking. I was sixteen this autumn and come of age—"

The master butted in. "Only God knows your true age, Ezra. It was an estimate, from your height and the length of your bones, and how your teeth had come on. Birthdays are a luxury for the rich or for those with the comfort of family. When I bought you in Spanish Town you had neither."

"I know that, sir. I have heard the story very many times. I do wonder that I can't remember my life before, not one single thing, not any sale or any transaction. Nothing."

"It is not unnatural. We tend to bury bad experiences, memories. Otherwise they can hurt us, make us bitter."

Ezra nodded. "I wanted to ask…"

"Is this about your people? We all want to know our provenance, lad. I wish to God that I could tell you more." Mr McAdam shook his head. "I doubt whether your mother would be alive. Those plantations work a man

– and woman – to the ground." He sighed. "Why society believes it allowable to treat the living as disposable but thinks our quest for vital knowledge akin to devilry is beyond—"

"I know, sir," Ezra cut in. "I know I had a lucky escape. It could have been worse for me in very many ways." He thought of his scar and the tumour on the shelf in the master's museum. "It is something else."

"Out with it, then, lad!"

"You have done so much for me, sir. But I think it is time I was independent. I have no means…"

"Ezra, lad, your skills will be your means. Don't you see that? Once you are fully trained—"

"But sir, you said I was better than most trained surgeons already!"

"Perhaps your head has swollen, Ezra, and I am to blame for it with too much praise." The master started towards the door that led back to the house. "Enough of this talk."

Ezra followed. "But sir! I am an adult! I need my own…"

"You will have in time, lad. Your impatience does you no favours!"

Ezra scowled at the master's back. He called after him, "I swear I have more than enough skill to work for the navy."

He should not have said it. The master turned round, furious, and strode back towards the table.

"The navy? I did not train you for butchery!" McAdam thumped the table and the body on it almost jumped. Ezra had heard him run down drunken navy surgeons over many dinners. It was the one thing guaranteed to draw a reaction. Now he wished he hadn't.

"No, sir." Ezra didn't look at him.

"Those navy sawbones! How many times have we seen how their work ends? Gangrene, stumps splintered and filthy. You are better than that! In a few years you will be a surgeon – I grant the mood these days means a mulatto surgeon may not raise the same fees as a white one, but, with my name, lad, you will be your own man."

"But I need to earn now!" Ezra burst out.

"You are more than an apprentice to me, lad." McAdam frowned. "The navy! Do not provoke me!"

Ezra turned away.

Mr McAdam put a hand on Ezra's shoulder and gently turned him about to face him. "I need you, Ezra. There is none your equal, none in the whole of London who knows how I like things done." He looked full into Ezra's eyes. "You are of age. And you are free. I would never wish to constrain you, but I wish you would think on it." McAdam looked away. "You know you are the son I never had. I beg you, think. Wait."

Ezra went to speak. He wanted to say how he knew McAdam was a fine master but how he wanted other things too; he wanted Anna, and he wanted to be his own man.

"The navy will be a harder life than you have known. I cannot stop you, but you would not have my blessing. A sensible lad such as yourself would not be so stupid."

"No, sir." Ezra felt trapped. He did not want to go to sea. He tried to think of some crystalline clear argument to advance his case for a wage.

"Mr Lashley offered me a paid position only yesterday."

"That fool? My boy, you are a better practitioner than him already. And he goes through apprentices the way the flux goes through a neighbourhood. You are too clever to work for him. Even if he paid you in Spanish gold!" Mr McAdam turned once again to leave. "I will have no more of this. Not a word. You have work to do and you will do it. And you can take a message to your Mr Lashley at Bart's. I must have words with him – he thinks to charge the poor for the Monday surgeries. But before that I would have you boil down and clean off the tibia belonging to the child – the left is the more bent, I think."

"Yes, sir." Ezra sighed. For the first time in his life he felt a deep irritation with his master. He was as tall as him now, eye to eye. And though he admired the man, right now he longed to storm out of his house and into the world.

Mr McAdam pulled on his jacket as if nothing had happened. He paused. "I'll ask Mrs Boscaven to make an Irish stew tonight. That is your favourite, if I am not mistaken."

"Sir! Please!" Ezra snapped. "I am a man. Do not seek to mollify me with treats like some lapdog!"

McAdam stepped back and there was silence between them. Ezra could see the hurt in his face.

Ezra felt angry and ashamed; he should not have spoken back to the master like that. He ran out into Ham Yard, still in his stained apron. He wanted to yell and rant and break something; feel the pain in his heart made real. He kicked a flowerpot against the wall and watched it shatter.

"Ooh, still upset, are you, bone boy?" Henry Toms was leaning against the wall smoking a clay pipe. He must have heard the exchange in the anatomy room. He grinned and tapped the old tobacco out of his pipe onto the ground. "Why don't you push off, like you want to? I'd be glad to see the back of you even if the master thinks you're worth feeding."

"Shut up, Toms."

"Don't tell me what to do, freak boy."

Ezra knew better than to let Toms needle him. Instead he imagined unpicking the cadaver's innards and flinging the three-day-old large intestine in the footman's face.

"What're you looking at now?" Toms said.

Ezra thought Toms was a lean streak of meanness and bitterness: why Mr McAdam kept him on was unfathomable.

"Nothing," Ezra said. He picked up the copper to boil the boy's bones and went back inside.

As he pared every scrap of flesh off the thigh bone he reflected that there was so much more trouble in the world than his own. This child, whose life had been brutal and short. The man, shot in his prime, perhaps for the price of his earrings. Ezra's own blood family, somewhere in Jamaica, on the far side of an ocean, breaking their backs cutting cane under the lash.

He lit a fire under the copper. Anna was as good as gone. He would have to live with it. This world was made of suffering, and if he didn't know that by now, he was no more than a child after all. The worst of it was, he knew McAdam was right. He would be better off in the long run if he stayed. He would never learn half as much with any other surgeon on earth. And he *would* be a good one. The best. That dream, at least, was still intact.

Ezra promised himself he would find the master as soon as he had completed his tasks, and apologize. But by the time Ezra went in to fetch the letter to take to Bart's, Mr McAdam had already left in a chair for a dinner at the Company of Surgeons and would not be back till late. It would have to wait.

As Ezra walked eastwards through the city, he did wonder why Mr Lashley wasn't going to be at the Company of Surgeons but surmised that any dinner he *was* at would be a much poorer and duller occasion.

He came to St Bartholomew's from the Old Bailey, holding his breath as he passed the massive stinking hulk of Newgate Prison, then up Giltspur Street and through the old gate of the hospital. As he turned under the archway he noticed a girl: small, maybe fourteen from her face, with bright – no, flaming – red hair piled on top of her head. She sat on a stool by the gateway, her arms folded, saying, doing nothing, only glaring. She was dressed in mourning, and the black of her dress and shawl only seemed to make the colour of her hair shout louder.

Ezra followed her line of sight. She was staring straight at the Fortune of War public house, which sat almost opposite the hospital entrance.

"Are you quite well, Miss?"

The watchman in his gatehouse shifted and stood up. "That'un's been there best part of the day. Not budged an inch," he said.

She was very still. Ezra waved a hand in front of her face.

"I am quite well, thank you. Now if you will leave me alone," she said, but did not look at him.

Ezra and the watchman exchanged looks. He tried again. "The Fortune of War is not a –" Ezra coughed, trying to find the word – "a very salubrious tavern."

"I done told her that already," the watchman put in.

At last the girl moved, turning her steely grey eyes on him. "Don't you think I know that, sir?"

Ezra shrugged; the girl obviously did not want his assistance. He turned and, with one last glance over his shoulder, made his way through the arch into the courtyard of the hospital and into the west wing, where Mr Lashley had his office.

As he walked along the first-floor corridor he looked out of the long window, which gave a perfect view of the corner of Giltspur Street and Cock Lane – and the tavern. He couldn't see the girl from here, but he was sure she was still there because, on the pavement outside the inn, a knot of men was standing, looking back towards where she had been sitting. Ezra recognized one of them as Mr Allen. Whatever the girl's fight was with those men, it was terribly one-sided. From her dress, Ezra guessed she had lost a loved one – perhaps those gentlemen had sold him on to surgeons.

Ezra thought he should like to tell her the truth of it, how they needed the cadavers to do their work, to find ways of making the living live longer, live better. But he knew it would be a waste of his time. He had had that conversation so many times and people never listened.

Ezra paused. He took a moment to brush down his

coat and pat his hair into place, then knocked twice on the door.

"Aha, Ezra McAdam! Changed your mind, I hope?" Mr Lashley sat behind an enormous dark wood desk. He was studying a jar containing an ear, and on his desk a pile of letters was held down with what looked like a twisted section of a human spine.

Lashley must have seen him looking. "Yes, rather fine, don't you think? It shows excessive osteophytes, bone spurs and scoliosis." He shook his head as if in wonder. "Quite remarkable."

"I have not given your offer any more thought, sir. I am quite happy where I am." Ezra kept his face blank. "My master sends you this." He took the letter out of his jacket.

"Is there a reply, sir?" Ezra asked, when he felt Lashley had had enough time to read it over. He would rather not wait while Mr Lashley composed an answer.

"No, not now. Although I would change Mr McAdam's mind. We do not operate for the good of the destitute!" Mr Lashley replied, waving him off as if he had more important things to do.

"As you wish, sir." Ezra nodded and left as quickly as he could. The man was a penny-pincher and no mistake. He hurried back down the stairs two at a time, glad to be making his way home.

Ezra could hear the commotion as soon as he came out into the hospital courtyard. At first he assumed an ox had escaped from a pen in Smithfield market – it happened often enough. But as he stepped out through the gate he could see it wasn't an ox that was being rounded up.

The men carried shovels and stakes. Allen was there, and a few of his company. They were chasing the girl, the one who'd been sitting stock-still – but she wasn't still now, not at all. She had her black skirts up and was running for her life, in and out of the animal pens of Smithfield market, falling and getting back up and jumping hurdles as fast as possible in full mourning. All the while the men bellowing and hollering, the sound bouncing and echoing off the hospital walls.

Ezra watched as she was cornered by two thickset resurrectionists, each with a shovel. The girl was half their size, width and breadth. Why was no one helping her? Ezra ran as fast as he could across the empty meat market.

As he dodged animals, he lost sight of her for a few minutes, but he followed the sounds of her furious shouting. Then came a scream, a sound of intense pain – a mirror of the sound the boy had made in the operating theatre the day before.

She was on the floor; one of the stakes that made up the animal pens stuck out of her thigh. Blood, dark as ink, pooled beneath her on the straw-covered ground.

"Leave her alone!" Ezra tried to sound in charge. "I am Ezra McAdam, apprentice to Mr William McAdam of Great Windmill Street." The men stepped back. He didn't recognize either man in the twilight, but they knew his name.

"Tell this harpy to leave us be or she'll get some more," one of them said. "Tell her!"

Ezra nodded. The men melted away.

The girl was writhing in pain. Ezra knelt down, took off

his neckerchief and tied it round her thigh. Then he put a finger into the pool of dark blood underneath her and sniffed. His face relaxed. It wasn't hers. Just some cow, perhaps, that had met its end in the same spot earlier.

"You!" The girl tried to push him away. "You're McAdam's man! I've heard that name. That butcher!" She still had enough fight to spit at him and he caught it in his face. "You will not kill me!"

Ezra wiped his cheek with his sleeve. "Correct. I will not."

"Then you'll not take my leg! Away, you gullion, you rusticutter!" She tried to get up and floundered, falling to the ground, her skirts awry. "Help me! Help!" she called into the empty market. Her face burned with fury and pain.

"I *am* the help," Ezra said. "And believe me, I have no wish to take your leg, or any other part of you."

He looked at her. She was uncommon in many ways; she did not look like a shop girl or a servant – she was too fierce. Her dress, though once expensive, was well worn, almost shabby. Most intriguingly, she spoke the words of the gutter in the voice of a lady.

"You are a visitor to the city?" he said.

She glared at him. "Hah! I am less of a visitor than you, sir! My people have lived here for…" She stopped. Ezra had pulled the hurdle out quickly and cleanly while she was distracted.

The girl burned the air so blue and so loud, Ezra imagined they could have heard every word as far away as Leicester Square. He checked the wound: it was deep, the cut at least an inch long, but the skin was not jagged. He must take care there were no splinters left inside. He needed light. She could not walk on it, so Ezra carried her across the market, in and out of the hurdles, until they were almost under the main gate. "Not Bart's, no!" the girl snarled. "My father went in alive and I never saw him again. I am not setting one foot inside!"

"Then truly," Ezra said as calmly as possible, "if you do not, you will only have one foot."

"Oh, I hate you!"

Ezra sighed. "I am not entirely well disposed to you either, though you are in need of help." She made a face. "Let me make myself clear. I will take you into the receiving ward. I will stitch up your wound. You could get another to do it, but I can say, honestly, that there are not many who would do as good a job as me. You would only have a bigger scar, it would take longer and it would cost you. From your dress, I'd venture to say that although you may be comfortable, you're not so wealthy you can afford a surgeon with stitches any better or neater than mine. I doubt you are swimming in cash. Or I could leave you here, and who knows? The wound might never close. The choice is yours."

She looked at him, her lip trembling. She was truly afraid, all her bravery had gone. Ezra sighed; he should not have been so cruel. A surgeon needed a good manner as well as a steady hand. He softened.

"It will be all right," he told her. "You did not lose so much blood. I think the larger measure was from an ox who'd had the stall before you. I will sew the wound. It will heal."

The girl said nothing. Ezra nodded at the porter as they went under the gate towards the receiving ward.

She wouldn't need a bed, Ezra thought, just a needle and suture. It was busy, as usual, and the smell was close to that in the master's anatomizing room. He saw the girl screw up her face.

"I think that is the smell of death," she said.

Ezra knew she was right, so he lightened his tone. "What is your name?"

"Miss Finch. And I know yours!" She laughed, bitterly. "You have his name – a butcher's name. A man known across the city for his anatomizing! If I were you I should change it."

Ezra ignored her and put her down carefully. He was well known around the hospital; a nursing sister found him a chair and he begged some suture and a needle from Mr Lashley's apprentice.

Miss Finch refused a draught of laudanum to calm her down. "On account that you'll have put something in it and I'll wake up on the table being dissected!"

"That will not happen. Unless you faint away through pain you will be quite awake – although I would advise you to look away. The thought of the deed is worse than the actuality."

"I want my wits about me, thank you very much." She glared at him.

Ezra had to tell her ten times to keep still, then, as quickly as he could, made four tiny stitches. Miss Finch bit her lip and looked away at first, but Ezra caught her watching and her face seemed to have changed from outrage to interest.

"There." He stood back. "If you hadn't wriggled so, I might have got in five smaller, but that will do."

"Pleased with yourself, aren't you?" she said. "I bet my stitches would be neater than yours."

He smiled. "I'd like to see that."

"I would say a human is no different from a smocked shirt. And I do the best smocked shirts – my pa said so…" Her voice tailed off.

"I'm sorry, Miss," he ventured into the silence that followed.

"No matter," Miss Finch said briskly, and got up to walk.

"No." Ezra put a hand out to stop her. "No pressure on it. Not for a few days. Not at all!"

"So I mightn't walk now?" She sounded worried.

"I'll bandage it up, but you will need to use a stick or a crutch," he told her. "Look, lean on me and we'll see if we can find the stores – there is bound to be one there." He stopped, seeing the shocked look on her face. "Just for a few days," he added hastily, "until the skin knits back together."

Miss Finch leant her shoulder against his and hobbled down the corridor past the medical wards. The lamps were all lit now, but it was a gloomy place, Ezra thought. There was crying and moaning, and perhaps the remembrance of hundreds of years of crying too.

"So many people have died here," Miss Finch said, as if reading his thoughts.

It wasn't long before they came to a cupboard full of sticks and trolleys and crutches. Ezra found her one of a suitable size and they left the hospital via the north gate.

"So you have no further opportunity to stir up the drinkers at the Fortune of War," he said.

"Those men are not ordinary drinkers."

"I know."

"And I know I have accomplished nothing with my vigil." She sighed. "I had hoped to make them feel something. Guilt, perhaps."

"The resurrectionists are not known for their tender feelings," Ezra said and she almost laughed.

"I have been an idiot. But since Pa died…"

"I am sorry. For your loss," Ezra said, thoughtful. "But in my line of work death is common; everyday. Sometimes I think it is more ordinary than life."

"Then I pity you. A life amongst the dead! No wonder you speak like an old man, though I swear you cannot be more than seventeen."

Ezra said nothing, he was pleased she thought him slightly older than his years.

"I know I said some terrible things to you, but you should know my reasons." She took a deep breath. "My father sickened and died within three days. It was so sudden. He was quite well until we returned home, the performance had been a complete success—"

"Performance?"

"We work as magicians. Falcon and Finch," she said. "My father is – was – Mr Charles Finch."

"Falcon and Finch!" Ezra smiled. "I saw you at Vauxhall last summer. Of course – and you are the Spirit of Truth! You could tell when men lied or spoke true. You and Mr Finch were a marvellous turn. Now I think of it, I even recall the hair. Anna thought you were quite splendid." Ezra paused, made a face. "Mr Falcon and his Italian cards, less so. I should so like to know how it all works."

"I cannot tell." Miss Finch's eyes sparkled with something like mischief. "Not on my life. Conjuror's honour. But thank you," she added. "I quite enjoyed being the Spirit of Truth. We haven't done that turn since last summer, we were thinking of ways to better it, improve on it." She sighed. "That will not happen now. I suppose my life will change more than I can know." She stared into the distance and Ezra thought she might cry. They walked on in silence. Ezra looked sideways at her. A performer. No wonder she had not fit into any of the categories he could think of. A magician's assistant! He had always wondered how those deceptions worked. Still, she looked sad now, and Ezra decided he preferred to see her fierce than sad. He should say something.

"So will you not continue to work with Mr Falcon?"

"Perhaps. He has been good to us. To me. He was a friend of my father's since before I was born. He has many contacts. I might go abroad, or work up my own act. But without father..."

"Tell me what happened to your father," Ezra said.

"He woke up poorly last Thursday, pale as..." She paused. "He was sick, vomiting all morning. I took him to the hospital. I should have stayed with him but I left him there – here. He told me he would be all right. And then he wasn't. I knew it was not natural, I would swear on all God's creatures above and below. But not a soul would listen. The final straw was that someone else came and claimed the body for burial! A woman, who said she was his sister. My father has no sister! Mrs Gurney, my landlady, said I should leave things be, but I cannot!" She was getting agitated again. Ezra thought of his stitches and sat her down on a bench in the courtyard.

"Oh, I know a thing or two about resurrectionists," Miss Finch went on. "I have heard what they do. I would give two guineas to prove that my father was murdered, and that he lies in the cellar of the Fortune of War."

"Two guineas?" Ezra's mind was racing. That would be more than enough to travel. His own funds. He could get a boat to Holland and back with that! He began to map out a plan of action. Why, he could walk across the road this minute and check to see if her pa was there, in the cellar.

"I have the money," the girl continued. "Well, I have Father's clothes and props. He will not need them now. The mad thing is," she said, looking at Ezra, "if they'd have asked me – once he was dead, that is – if your lot had come and said nicely, 'Look, Loveday, we can help you, we can tell you why your Pa died,' I'd have said, 'You know what? The man's dead, so, yes, why not?'" She took a breath. "Pa loved science, he wouldn't have minded being sat next to the Irish Giant, up in your man's museum, with a little sign round his neck saying Skeleton of the World's Greatest Magician."

"Your name is Loveday?"

"What of it?"

"Nothing. Unusual." Like its owner, Ezra thought. He turned to her and declared, "I will take the job. I will find your father's corpse, and I will find the cause of his death."

"You could do that?" She smiled – properly this time, her eyes alight with new hope. Ezra looked at her. He remembered her all in white, almost like a Grecian, on stage as the Spirit of Truth in Vauxhall Gardens.

He smiled back at her. "Yes," he said. "I think I could."

Chapter Three

The Fortune of War Public House
Giltspur Street
London
November 1792

Ezra called a cab for Miss Loveday Finch, and as it turned out of sight he thought on his next actions. Already the notion that he might earn some decent cash, do a lady a favour and solve a riddle all at once was opening up an exciting range of possibilities.

He had often thought that the anatomist's skills were especially useful in post-mortem examinations – better than those of a doctor, who was, after all, no more than an apothecary who treated only surface and appearance. A cadaver was always a puzzle, but usually the reasons for death were mundane and clear: poverty, old age, drowning, cold, malnutrition. If Miss Finch was telling the truth about her father – and of course there was the possibility her mind was moved to imaginings by grief – then this might be a very interesting way to pocket some rhino.

Ezra had told her to go home, not to disturb her father's room – he would go over there tomorrow, after work, and take a close look – and to live her life as entirely without remark as possible. If there had been a murder, and it was not the random assault and robbery kind, then Ezra was sure the murderer would be known to both Miss Finch and her father. On the few occasions he had discussed murder with Mr McAdam, the master had said he was of the opinion that most who died in a violent and sudden way did so at the hands of someone close to them: the wronged wife, the vicious husband, the unwanted child.

As he stood in the street he heard the church at St Sepulchre chime for eight o'clock. He needed to be back at the house for Mr Allen and his company to pick up the things, ready and waiting in the anatomy room. But perhaps Allen would be sitting in the Fortune of War now, drinking before his evening's work? It would be simple enough to find out.

Ezra had never before set foot inside such a low dive. The place was known to be dangerous. It was said that in the cellar there was a room set out with shelves all around the walls. Not bookshelves, but shelves for cadavers ready to be sent all over London to this or that anatomy or medical school. Ezra counted them off inside his head. He knew of ten private schools like the master's, and then there were the hospital schools, Bart's and Guy's and St Thomas's, Middlesex and St George's. They all needed corpses to learn from, to practise on, yet the trade – and it was definitely a trade – was entirely corrupt. The world, Ezra thought, was a very contrary place.

He looked up at the tavern again. How should he play it – breeze in, asking to see their wares? Was that what one did? One thing was sure: Ezra was far more afraid of the living than the dead. He walked past once, twice, then pushed in through the door before he could change his mind.

Inside, the tavern was a fug of tobacco smoke. That and the yellow candlelight made it hard to see anything at first. He had worried all eyes would swivel to look at him as he entered, but that was practicably impossible. The place was too busy, too noisy: a violin scraped out a tune, a choir of drunken voices caterwauled along. A couple of boys danced out a rhythm in wooden shoes.

The air was thick with smells: ale, spirits, hot pies, but mostly unwashed men and damp. A hard place to have a good time, Ezra would have thought. He made it to the bar, where a legend painted in gold and black read: WE KNOW NOT THE DAY NOR THE HOUR.

The drinkers were a mix of medical students that Ezra recognized from St Bart's, Smithfield market workers, a few snotter-haulers and second-hand clothes traders, and the resurrection men. He spotted a couple of Allen's cronies and, in the corner at the back, the man who'd chased Miss Finch, glaring ten kinds of holy death at him.

Ezra took a deep breath. The only way he could see was to ask outright if the thing was here and then do whatever it was Mr McAdam did: enquire about the purchase of the thing and persuade them to deliver it to Great Windmill Street on the master's account. If any of the resurrectionists did him any real harm, he told himself, the master would hear of it. That fact alone was his protection. What he would tell the master if and when an extra delivery was made – well, he would have to cross that bridge when he came to it.

The man in the corner was still staring at him, so Ezra

bought him a drink at the bar and walked over. He had no option but to cut directly to the chase and see what followed.

"Good evening," Ezra said, setting down the pot tankard in front of him.

"And to you, young McAdam." The man paused, sniffed, took a drink. "Mr Allen says you're a straight cove, is it true?"

"I'd like to think so, yes." Ezra sat down across the table from him.

"So how's your lady friend?'

"She's not so much of a friend. It's simply business."

"Ah," said the man, "business. My favourite." He sat back, inviting Ezra to speak.

"I'm looking for something. Some *thing* in particular. But I'll need to check it over first."

"Some … thing?" the man answered. "Where I'm from, south of the river," he said quietly, "we like to think of them as cold meat. Fresher the better, of course. Sometimes they're parcels. Packets. Special deliveries."

Ezra had heard those terms too. He nodded.

"Well, I'm sure we can provide what you need, young sir. Even in such times as these when the world and his wife are looking for … *things*." The man leant close, and Ezra could smell the stench of his breath. "We have your address, delivery tomorrow morning?"

"No." Ezra coughed. "It's a particular thing I need. I have to see them." He lowered his voice. "I need to see their faces."

The man scowled. "And play them a tune while you're at it!" His voice was low and threatening. He swore.

"Know this: if you weren't McAdam's boy I'd have you thrown out in the street on your arse." He finished his drink and stood up, motioning Ezra to follow, and they left the bar and stepped behind a curtain through a door. He picked up and lit a candle stub, and Ezra followed him down some steep stone steps. The smell and the cold hit him on the second step. The familiar, summer-sweet, sick-sour smell of death. It was so heavy that Ezra felt the vomit rise up from his stomach.

The man grinned. "Not used to it, are you, lad?"

Ezra would have liked to dispute the fact and say, yes, he was completely used to the human body, most especially when it was deceased. But this was different: the smell was turned here into something almost solid. He had to put his hand out to the wall to steady himself; it felt wet and cold as ice and shocked the sickness out of him.

The room was low-ceilinged, but contrary to the rumour there were no shelves for the bodies to lie prone and stately in their sacks. Here the sacks were higgledy-piggledy, against every wall. Ezra counted eight – they'd be worth a small fortune. One or two had obviously been here longer than others; even in the candlelight he could make out the damp patches, large and spreading. He tried to stop himself imagining how far the decomposition must have gone.

"I think this is the one you want," the man said, and opened a sack nearest the door. "Freshest. Like he's just fell asleep." Ezra could see the corpse's grey hair, and he shook his head quickly.

The man shrugged and opened another. A woman. Ezra shook his head again.

"Well, the others all have takers. This is Mr Lashley's." The man tugged the sacking down over the cadaver's face. "He's special, in a way – found abandoned, he was, like luggage."

That was him, Mr Charles Finch. Ezra nodded. The hair was a giveaway, darker red than the girl's but thick and curly; the nose long and straight and the chin sharp, just as she had described. But there was no way in hell he could tell whether the cove had suffered violence in any way, not down here in this dim light, with this stench.

"How's that? I thought he was retrieved from the hospital? The old 'dead sister' trick," Ezra said, and regretted speaking, for the smell was so tangible and solid, it was as if he'd swallowed a mouthful of the foul air.

"Would we do a thing like that?" The man smiled. "No, this poor lamb was left in the graveyard of St Sepulchre's by the meat market, thrown over the wall." He shrugged.

Ezra thought that very odd – but then, he told himself, resurrectionists were not known for their truth-telling.

"Could you get Mr Allen to deliver him to Great Windmill Street?" he asked, before remembering the stink.

"I told you, this'un's Mr Lashley's, and the man keeps us sweet and regular on a retainer," the man said. "Of course if you were to offer a tidy sum and find me a suitable replacement double quick…"

Ezra's heart sank. How would he square it with the master, paying double for a very ordinary cadaver? And where did the man expect him to find another body at such short notice? He had to find another way.

"When's it going?" Ezra tried not to open his mouth too much.

"I ain't telling you any more without an ounce in my hand, young sir."

"Five shillings!" Ezra choked out. "I'll give you two – it's all I have."

He handed over the coins and the man grinned. "It's going tonight. Lecture's in the morning, I expect."

Ezra backed up the stairs two at a time. "And thank you for your time," he called down after him. Then he dashed out into the street and gulped down the fresh air as if it were Mrs Boscaven's finest lemon cordial. He ran all the way back to High Holborn and home, glad, even running through the dark, to be out of that place.

He would have to get himself into Lashley's demonstration in the morning, he thought to himself as he ran. Before he sought out Miss Finch at her address in Bloomsbury. He'd need to see the body up close. He'd have to talk to Josiah – Lashley's apprentice and, unlike his master, a decent sort – and see what he could do.

Poor Loveday. He resolved not to tell her. Even the dead deserved a better end than Lashley.

It was past nine when he reached Great Windmill Street, but Ezra thought he would wait up for Mr McAdam. If he was in a merry mood after the surgeon's dinner there would be no better time to apologize for his outburst this morning. Mrs Boscaven made him ginger tea and Ezra took it into the anatomy room to wait for Mr Allen. He sat down on one of the student's benches and as he sipped his tea his mind went to the fate of the two people now stowed in sacks – one on the table, the other, the smaller, on the trolley.

There were so many ways a human child could die. In fact, he thought, it was more of a miracle that anyone made it to adulthood.

As for the other one... Mr Finch's death might be a puzzle, but this body surely posed the greater riddle. Ezra put down his teacup and went over to the sack. He untied it and looked one more time at the tattoo on the man's inner forearm. He took out his notebook and pencil from his apron pocket and tried to copy the mark, but even in the last glimmerings of candlelight it was not easy. Allen would be here before it was done. On an impulse, Ezra put down his notebook, took a knife and cut an oblong of skin away around the mark. He put the skin flat between the last pages of his notebook. After all, it might mean something.

No member of Mr McAdam's household ventured into the anatomy room if they could help it, so after Mr Allen had been and picked up the bodies, Ezra yawned and stretched out on one of the benches, looking up at the stars through the glass roof. It had been a long day. What was Anna doing, he wondered – preparing to leave? Or perhaps she was looking at the stars too, and thinking of him. Perhaps he would find time to see her tomorrow...

Ezra didn't realize he had fallen asleep until the full moon shining down through the glass roof woke him up. That and the sound of cats fighting in the yard. He sat up – his shoulder hurt from sleeping on the hard bench. He rubbed at it, swung his arm round trying to loosen up the joint. He was cold, too. He looked up at the house, all was dark. He must have missed the master arriving home and going up to bed.

That was when he heard another sound. Someone was trying to get in through the yard door, turning the handle, twisting it – softly at first, a light click, then, as it failed to give, rattling it harder. Ezra hadn't yet drawn the bolts. If they picked the lock they'd be through in an instant.

He felt his heart racing, then he heard a voice outside the door. Someone cursed and dropped something metal, he heard it go bouncing over the stone cobbles of the yard. If it was just one man he could take him down, couldn't he? But the master's tools, the knives and the saws, were locked in the cupboard under the table. Ezra cursed silently; the key was on a hook in the master's laboratory. All he had was the broom, propped up against the door leading into the house. He could use that. Ezra prayed that the cove outside trying his damnedest to break in didn't have a blade. Or a pistol.

Slowly, Ezra slid off the bench and across the floor. Every sound seemed ten times louder. He could hear the leather in his shoes creak, and the silver moonlight lit his every move brighter than a hundred candles.

Another voice. Ezra froze, strained his ears to listen.

"Hurry it up, man." The voice was clear. Whoever spoke did not sound like Ezra's idea of a regular cracksman. Foreign, perhaps. "It's not the dead that can hurt you! Come on, before the place wakes up."

Ezra heard a grunted reply. There were at least two of them, then. He took another step towards the broom, slipped on a stray branch of bay and fell heavily to the floor, taking the empty trolley over with him. His fall made a crack and a thump loud enough, he thought, to shatter every pane of glass in the roof.

There was more cursing from the yard, and then footsteps – they were off. One of them had nails in his boots – Ezra heard them tattooing a rhythm out of the yard, into Great Windmill Street and away down to the Haymarket.

Ezra lay there for a while, gritting his teeth against the pain he'd incurred falling awkwardly on his knee, grateful they'd gone. He got up, turned the trolley over and, cautiously, even though he was sure they had gone, opened the door to the yard. The cold hit the back of his throat and made the bare skin on his arms prickle. His breath formed clouds as he looked around. The yard was empty. Even Mrs Perino's chickens were safe in their coop. He went back inside and drew all the bolts.

The house hadn't stirred. Mrs Boscaven, Ellen and the master had slept through it all. He hadn't imagined it, had he? He took a candle into Mr McAdam's office at the front of the house and opened the shutters a crack but the street was empty.

Ezra made his way up the stairs, through the museum and into his room, hoping the house crackers weren't about to return before the morning.

As he lay in bed there were so many thoughts flying round his head it took a full hour before he dropped back to sleep. The Finch girl and her father, the scene in the cellar at the Fortune of War, Anna away to Holland within a week, Mr Lashley's offer, the tongueless cadaver and those two cracksmen trying to break in. Ezra turned over, tried to get comfortable in his bed, to think of nothing.

Those men could just be ken crackers or sky-larkers,

filled up with one too many jars of ale, looking for an easy earner – or better still, simple bluey hunters looking to take the lead off the glazed roof. But if they were, they'd have had a ladder. And then they wouldn't have known there might be bodies. They were here for a reason. Perhaps the Negro killed by gunshot *was* important? But if that was so, wouldn't the fact be all over the papers? Whatever the cause Ezra knew he must talk with the master. First thing.

The fire was lit in the grate when he woke up. Ellen had been and gone and he had slept through it all. Ezra jumped out of bed. He couldn't see the clock on St Anne's from his bedroom, but there was one in the museum – he had to hurry, ask the master for leave to attend Mr Lashley's lecture. He pulled on his clothes and dashed through into the museum. It was eight thirty; he could still get to St Bartholomew's in time.

He knocked on Mr McAdam's door and pushed it open. He could only see the man's back and hear the sound of his pen scratching away. Another paper for the Company of Surgeons, Ezra supposed, or details of the unusual cadavers they'd dealt with yesterday. His master was a great one for records.

"Excuse me, sir…"

"Don't disturb me now, Ezra!" Mr McAdam didn't even turn around. "I have a busy day and must finish these notes before breakfast. And if you were wondering if I need you today, the answer is no. As long as the museum is in order and your work is too."

"Yes, sir, but…"

"You are dismissed, then."

Ezra shut the door. He would tell Mrs Boscaven about the attempted break-in and perhaps she could get Toms to check the locks and fit some new ones. Although getting Toms to do anything was as easy as teaching cats to call in Latin. Ezra fetched his heavy worsted jacket. The clouds promised snow and plenty of it.

By the time Ezra pushed his way into the crowded lecture theatre, the cadaver that had been Mr Charles Finch was flat on the table. There was a four-inch cut across his belly, but Mr Lashley was now slicing the right arm. The skin had been pulled back and the tendons and main arteries were displayed in a sort of asymmetrical fan; the bones of his forearm and hand, free of flesh, shone white.

But Ezra could see Lashley had cut crudely, flesh and tendon were mixed in with the sawdust on the floor. A few of the keener students hung on Mr Lashley's every word, and Ezra felt a little sorry for those of them who had never experienced Mr McAdam's superior knifework.

Mr Lashley had got his position, Ezra had heard, because his own father had been surgeon general at St Thomas's on the south side of the river. Unfortunately, although Mr Lashley had followed in his brilliant father's footsteps, it was clear he did not have the same talent or skill.

Ezra craned forward as far as he could in order to study the veins and arteries; they had a healthy colour, no obvious sign of poison or anything else unnatural. But there were so many people in the crush of the lecture room, he wondered how he would get to have a really good look.

He waited until the lecture was over and the students

had departed. Ezra watched Mr Lashley take off his apron and nod towards Josiah.

"Ezra McAdam, twice in as many days!" Mr Lashley said, putting on a very fine embroidered coat. "Another letter, perhaps, from your master?"

"No, sir. I just heard you would be concentrating on the brachial and the *profunda brachii* arteries." Ezra coughed. "A special interest of mine, sir."

"Indeed! I hope I filled any gaps in your knowledge left by Mr McAdam."

"Thank you, sir. And if you don't mind, could I speak with Josiah for a minute?"

"Of course – but no plotting, boys, no plotting." Lashley smiled at his own joke. "And Josiah, clear this one away and then see me after luncheon in my office. You have a good deal of work you haven't finished since Friday!"

Josiah nodded. Mr Lashley swept out in his new coat.

"I would give all the gold in Spain for that old sawbones to swap places with this here cadaver," Josiah grumbled. "Old man Lashley would find fault with a fat goose." He looked up from his work. "If I could, I would join the army, take the king's shilling, like that." He clicked his fingers. "Your old man hasn't got a position going, has he? You've no plans to sail into the sunset?"

"Oh, I am most definitely staying put," Ezra said, smiling. He didn't mention that yesterday he'd been foolish enough to consider leaving. Seeing Josiah here, he realized how lucky he was.

"I could help you clean up if you like," Ezra offered. He could see the gobbets of flesh and fat in the sawdust, and the dirty instruments. Josiah looked relieved.

"So, what are you up to, Ez? Not that I couldn't do with a hand or two to clean this lot up." Josiah grinned and waved Mr Finch's almost-severed hand.

"Jos! Leave it out!" Ezra objected and Josiah put the hand down with a shrug. "If I help you," Ezra went on, picking up the broom, "you can let me have a good look at your specimen."

"Friend of yours, is he?"

"Never met the man. But I saw him escape from several pairs of knuckle dabs at Vauxhall Gardens last summer."

"A conjuror, then? A good one?"

Ezra nodded.

Jos smiled. "Didn't escape death, though, did he."

"If he could do that he'd have earnt a lot more." Ezra swept the sawdust up into a heap. "Tell me, Jos – you've had a good look at this one. Anything odd strike you? Anything rum about it?"

Josiah shrugged. "It's like any other – fresh, clean. One thing, though: some cove had opened the stomach cavity up already. Could be a professional from the cleanness of the cut, although, given as I'm used to old Lashley, it might not have been. See? Taken the stomach and most of the intestine, they have."

Ezra put the broom down and had a look. He thought it must have happened after death and before the body had been abandoned in the graveyard. "There's a rum turn-up and no mistake."

Josiah nodded and flapped open the stomach. "My thoughts exactly. See, empty as a pauper's pocket."

Ezra furrowed his brow. If it were poison, where was

his proof now? Perhaps that's why it had been taken, but who would care? Lashley wouldn't. "Who would take a stomach?" Ezra said it aloud.

"Search me," Jos said. "First one I've ever seen cut out like that, and you and me, we've seen it all. Remember the man they cut open at St Thomas's with the thing inside him, teeth an' all? I had nightmares for a week after that."

"But this is no growth, Jos. Somebody took it out on purpose. Whoever did this was trying to hide something."

"Or maybe looking for something." Jos smiled. "Last night's dinner?"

"So it was you, Jos! Mr Lashley keeping you hungry, is he?"

"Your wit wants a deal of sharpening, Ez!" Jos fetched a bonesaw. "Oh, and Mr Lashley never opened his chest," Josiah said, "so he won't mind if I do it now and save him the trouble."

Mr Finch had been tall, six foot, Ezra guessed, although once a man was dead you never could tell how he had stood when living: stooped, hunched or proud and tall. He was broad, too, and not too far past his prime; Ezra guessed his age at forty. But his heart – or rather the poor, shrivelled thing that sat inside him – looked incapable of pumping blood around a man half his size. The two boys stared hard.

"Heaven's name! That is unnatural and no mistake!" Josiah said, shaking his head and whistling low. "I've never seen the like…"

"Nor me," Ezra agreed, looking closer. "Never in all my born days!"

Chapter Four

Mrs Gurney's Lodging House
Clerkenwell Green
London
November 1792

Ezra promised Josiah a drink and a fish supper in return for what remained of Mr Charles Finch. Then he took the wizened little heart away in one of Mr Lashley's specimen jars and put it into his cloth shoulder bag. Perhaps, he thought as he passed the shining white new museum in Bloomsbury, the condition had affected him for years; perhaps whatever had caused the damage was an illness. Or perhaps it was something else, something as yet undiscovered. Mr McAdam would be most interested to see this heart. All arguments would be forgotten, Ezra was certain.

He called in at an undertaker's and arranged for Mr Finch's body to be taken in a sealed coffin to Loveday's address. Her father would be delivered into the bosom of his family and she would have her funeral. He felt so pleased with himself at the outcome that he went to call on her straight away. She was bound to be glad he had made such progress, and perhaps even forward a half of the two guineas she had promised.

Miss Finch's lodgings were at Clerkenwell Green, just on the northern edge of the city, in a terrace, some of the houses so old they leant against one another like happy drunks. Ezra wondered if a girl who lived here could afford the two guineas she had promised him or if it were all some wild goose chase. It must be a strange life, he thought to himself, being a performer, a conjuror – moving from town to town, seeing the world but owing one's existence to pretence and artifice rather than flesh and blood.

There were a couple of newer houses in the row, and he was relieved to find that Number 52 was one of these, not entirely blackened by grime, and with fine oblong windows in the modern style. He looked up, and in the first-floor window he could see Miss Finch staring out. When she saw him she smiled, her sharp features softening. Ezra waved up at her, and saw the winter sunlight glance off what must be a blade in her hand: a rapier or duelling sword. She swished it to and fro and looked as if she could do real damage with the weapon. Ezra decided it would not be to his advantage to mention what he carried in his bag – the only blades he was any use with were the surgeons' variety.

The woman who answered the door was dressed in pale grey rather than mourning black, hair scraped back under a starched white bonnet. The landlady, Ezra decided, rather than family. Her expression was as sour as a bowl full of lemons.

"I am Mrs Gurney." She looked Ezra up and down most thoroughly. "And you, I assume, are Ezra McAdam. Miss Finch told me to expect you. Although I do not think it at

all right a young lady should admit callers unchaperoned."
Her voice was clipped and cold.

Loveday Finch stood at the top of the stairs, leaning
on the banister rail. "Send him up, please, Mrs Gurney,"
she called down. "This is none but my own business."

The landlady pursed her lips and stood back. "I will
say nothing, then," she answered tightly. "Though I
do not like foreigners in my house." And with that she
swished away down the basement stairs. Ezra would have
liked to tell her he was hardly foreign, having lived more
than two-thirds of his life in this city, but he knew there
was little point.

"Take no notice," Loveday Finch said as she led him
into the drawing room. Although she wore mourning,
Ezra thought she looked more determined than grieving.

"Your leg is healing?" he asked.

"But not my heart, Mr McAdam. I thought you might
send word earlier. I have been waiting."

"It's not yet noon, Miss Finch." Ezra was about to tell
her the good news but found himself staring at the acid
yellow walls of the drawing room.

"Mrs Gurney is fond of bright colours. I do not think
a shade like this exists in nature." Loveday laughed.
"I know she is severe but she has been good to us – to
me," she said. "How is your blade hand? I have been
practising. I have had nothing to do but think of ways I
could have stopped Pa dying. I should have helped him!
Done something, surely…" She swished her blade deter-
minedly. Ezra could see she was about to cry. She was an
odd girl, he thought: brave and bold on the surface but all
tears and strange fancies underneath.

"Miss Finch, please, do not worry so. I have found your father and he will be delivered to you tomorrow. You may proceed with the funeral."

"Oh! Thank heavens." Her face relaxed.

"And you should not be on your feet. Your wound needs to heal." He could see the furniture had been pushed to either side of the room, leaving a considerable clear space in the centre – for her sword practice, Ezra supposed.

"Such welcome news! Mr McAdam, if I offended you last night, forgive me. Oh, Pa is coming home!" She swished the sword again. "I will have to see the rector at St James's and write to Pa's friends." She wiped her face and smiled.

"Here." She offered him a blade. "I think better when I am doing something."

Ezra's hands tightened on his bag; he was loath to put it down just so that Loveday might swing a sword at him. She noticed his hesitation and tapped it with her blade. "What have you in there that you guard it so closely, the crown jewels?"

"I didn't come here to learn fencing, Miss," Ezra replied stiffly. "I have been working for you, earning my fee, which I hope you can pay."

Loveday blanched. For a moment, against the black mourning and the yellow walls, her skin looked so pale as to be almost green, and Ezra regretted the mention of money.

"Excuse me, Miss Finch. I ought not to have spoken so. Please sit down."

"No, I am quite well. You will have your money, but you may have to wait until his accounts are clear." She straightened. "Now, a little sport." She swished her blade and almost keeled over. Ezra steered her towards a seat.

"I am sorry," she said. "I cannot stand this! Pa always said each of us must make our own future. Now it seems as if I am waiting for the future to decide what it will do with me. You will have to forgive me if I am not used to it."

She was so pale that Ezra took her hand and felt her pulse, which was racing under the skin at her wrist. She pulled away.

"Miss Finch, I am not some Sunday suitor, I am a doctor." Ezra pulled her hand back. "You need to rest. It is imperative."

"But I cannot! I think of nothing but Pa, I swear something happened to him – his death came from the blue. He was quite well; quite healthy. Have you discovered what caused his death? Did those men dispatch him?"

Ezra hesitated for a second. He couldn't tell her about the heart.

"You think something is fishy about this too, don't you?"

"Miss Finch, I cannot say…"

"You do! It is written all over your face that you think his death unnatural! You forget I was the Spirit of Truth and can read your thoughts right off your face. I should find those ressurectionists and they should swing for my father. Tell me their names!"

"Miss Finch, stealing a corpse is not an actual crime."

"Is that the law?" Loveday said, surprised.

Ezra nodded. "And in any case, I have reason to believe it was not resurrectionists who took your father's body from Bart's."

"Who, then?" She made a face. "How did he die?"

"I only saw the cadaver briefly," he told her. "I could not tell how he died."

Miss Finch almost gasped. "You saw him! How did he look? Peaceful?"

Ezra looked away in case she really could read his mind. "He was dead, Miss. All the dead are peaceful. I have many questions to ask."

"Then ask."

Ezra put the bag on his lap and took out his notebook carefully. "Your father's heart. Did he complain of pains? Could he walk from here to, say, Covent Garden, without pain?"

"Of course. He never complained of any pain. Ever."

"You are sure?"

She nodded. "Certainly."

"Then could you please tell me the events that preceded his death."

"I told you, he was quite well…"

Ezra shook his head. "No, I need details. I need everything from the day before, from when you first thought he might be ill—"

"You *do* think he was murdered, don't you!"

"Perhaps, Miss Finch – I cannot commit to an opinion quite yet."

"Very well. Although nothing happened out of the ordinary. Nothing at all. And how far back should I go? The performance on Monday night? Mrs Gurney's inexcusable fish paste sandwiches that afternoon? Our return from Constantinople barely a fortnight ago?"

"You were in Turkey recently?" Ezra said, surprised.

"Yes, we travel all about."

"The sandwiches, then – what was wrong with them? Did you eat them too?"

"Of course. I was hungry. They were awful, though. Mrs Gurney keeps a clean house, but her cook!" Loveday looked at Ezra. "Do you think Pa was—"

"I am endeavouring to keep an open mind," he cut in. "Now, Miss Finch, the facts!"

"We had tea, sandwiches and seed cake and then took a cab to St James's Square. It was a private performance at the offices of the Ottoman ambassador, Ali Pasha. You should see the size of the place! I swear only Devonshire House is larger."

Ezra wrote it all down.

"The performance was a success. I didn't see much of Pa afterwards, as he was talking to Mr Falcon and the envoy in the reception room. I was engaged in packing up our props. When I think of it now, Pa was already quite pale when we got in the cab to go home. I thought he was tired."

"And the vomiting began then?" Ezra prompted.

"Yes. He swore blind he was simply tired. He said he'd eaten too many of those pastries – baklava, they're called. We ate them in Constantinople all the time. Pa loved them. Pistachio nuts and honey."

"Pistachio nuts," Ezra said thoughtfully. "Are those the green ones? Did you eat any?"

"They had all gone by the time I came out of the dressing room." She gasped. "Was it the baklava?"

"I can't know yet. Please, tell me what happened next."

"We arrived home after midnight and Pa needed

a bucket because of the sickness. I woke Mrs Gurney, who wasn't pleased. I fetched him some water from the kitchen and he told me to go to bed, said he would be all right." She sighed.

"And in the morning?"

"We often woke late, but when Pa wasn't up by ten I knocked on his door…" Her voice trailed off. "That was when I took him to hospital."

"What was his condition, exactly?" Ezra asked. "Skin tone? Eyes, were they clear? Any difficulty breathing?"

"He was my father, not some kind of specimen!" Loveday Finch's voice was cracking. She looked at Ezra. "He was ill – very, very ill."

"I am sorry, Miss Finch, I need to know."

She said nothing, but stared out of the window for a long time. The sound of the clock on the mantelpiece seemed to cut the silence into bars.

"I suppose you do," she said after a long while. "Do you think it might have been the Turkish pastries?"

"Is there anyone at the Ottoman Embassy…?"

"Not at all. They love Falcon and Finch. In Constantinople we are favourites in the palace, especially with the ladies of the harem. They—"

"But I thought men were not allowed in the harem?" Ezra interrupted.

"Well, it was very strange. We played in a room that was quite empty save for some official. We could hear them – the ladies – but we weren't allowed to see them. They watched through a screen. They live entirely separate lives, you know, along with the children. In fact, Pa told me the male children, the heirs, have it especially hard. They are shut away in their own part of the palace – they call it the Cage. I know, so dramatic – and then when the old sultan pops it they pluck a new boy out. But sometimes these poor lads have spent so long alone they turn out quite mad."

"That's inhuman!" Ezra cried.

"It might just be rumour. Pa said there was so much intrigue at court, but the Turks I met were all as nice as pie. Nicer, indeed."

"In my experience, if someone is murdered, the murderer is usually someone from their own family."

Loveday got up. "I find it rather offensive that you assume his family – by which you mean me – has anything to do with Pa's death." She was glaring at him now. He stood up too. Perhaps he wouldn't ask for payment just yet.

"Miss Finch, that is not what I meant, not at all. I'm merely stating the truth, I didn't mean…"

Loveday glared at him. "Good."

"We must remember that your father's death may have been due to an existing illness. A weakness of the heart—"

"I doubt that," Miss Finch interrupted. "I would put money on it being murder. I feel it in my bones."

Ezra hid a smile. "I doubt that your bones are capable of such emotion, Miss Finch. Now, if we could see your father's bedroom."

"I don't know how helpful that will be," Loveday said. "Mrs Gurney has been in there with Gwen, the maid." But she led the way all the same.

Ezra followed her upstairs. She was so different from

any girl he had spoken with – although apart from Anna, that list was not long. He thought that if he was ever murdered he would want someone as bold and tenacious as Miss Finch to make certain justice was done.

Mr Finch's room was on the floor above. It had been tidied into submission, and not a trace of the man, of any man, remained. Only a good jacket, a couple of hats and a beautifully embroidered cloak, all tulips and roses and blue and red silk, hung up on the hook behind the door.

Miss Finch must have seen him looking. "It was a gift, from the valide sultan in Constantinople. She adored the act."

"Valide?"

"It's the title of the queen mother – well, the sultan's mother. She is French, you know. Stolen off a boat in the Atlantic by corsairs."

Ezra looked at her.

"I am not making up tales! I heard her speak of it. She spoke better French than the boys who rig the Alhambra in Paris." Loveday sighed. "Pa loved Constantinople." Her shoulders drooped a little. Ezra shut his notebook and went to put it in his bag – but it wasn't there.

At that moment there was a scream, loud and angry, from the floor below.

They raced downstairs. Mrs Gurney was standing at the far end of the yellow drawing room. Ezra's bag was open on the floor, and the jar with Mr Finch's heart had rolled along the floor and up to the landlady, pinning her against the fireplace. In the reflected yellow glow of the drawing-room walls it looked unearthly.

"Get it away!" Mrs Gurney squealed. "Get the thing away!"

Ezra quickly scooped it up. She must have opened his bag and gone through his things.

"What on earth *is* that?" asked Miss Finch.

Ezra looked at her. He was in the girl's drawing room holding her dead father's heart. His mouth felt like ashes. He couldn't speak.

Miss Finch moved closer.

"Is it a heart?" she said. Her voice wavered between repulsion and interest. "Is it a human heart?"

Mrs Gurney screamed again. "He is from hell!" She pulled Miss Finch away. "Get out!" she shouted at Ezra. "Get out, now! If I see you again I shall call the watch!"

Ezra had picked up his bag and run down the stairs and out into the street before he realized his good worsted jacket was still hanging in the hall. He would freeze before he got as far as High Holborn. His arms already tingling with cold, he set off down the road at quite a pace. Had the master said the Negro could have been a servant to some Eastern court? And now, here, was it more than a coincidence that Mr Finch had worked at the Ottoman Embassy?

The master would discount coincidence. Facts and science were all that could be relied upon, he would say. But these coincidences could not be ignored! The man without a tongue might be more important than they knew. Ezra should ask her about it now – after all, he would have to go back to fetch his jacket. As he turned back he saw the door of the house open and Miss Finch run out holding his coat.

"You forgot this!"

"Thank you, Miss Finch. Please, let me apologize. I never meant…"

"Do not worry, Mrs Gurney is afraid of her own shadow."

Ezra put his coat on. "Miss Finch, I must ask you—"

"Was that really a heart?" Miss Finch cut in, awestruck.

"Yes, but—"

"Whose was it? Did you cut it out?" She held her hands over where her own heart beat and lived. It made Ezra uncomfortable.

"It's my work, Miss Finch. I am sorry if I scared Mrs Gurney, but I need to ask you something, something important concerning your father's death."

"It was murder, no doubt at all, Mr McAdam."

Ezra had to admit he agreed, but the girl was so volatile, he must proceed carefully. If there were a suspect, he was sure she would take her blade and hobble off to avenge her father's death in an instant.

"Your father, you said he did a lot of work for the Ottoman court?"

"Yes. As I said, he was a favourite of the valide sultan – the sultan's mother. And in London we often worked at the embassy, at least once or twice a year when they had receptions for other ambassadors – important people. You know."

Ezra did not know, but he was not going to say. He cleared his throat.

"And in the Ottoman Embassy, was there anyone in particular your father corresponded with about work and such? A Negro, perhaps?"

Loveday shook her head. "Not a Negro, a Mr Ali Pasha. But there were servants about the place – some of them were Negroes. Why, what is it?"

"Nothing." Ezra sighed. He must not allow himself to jump to rash conclusions. "I must get back to work. I will inform you of my findings as soon as I am ready. Goodbye, Miss Finch." He bowed slightly and began to walk away.

"I say, Mr McAdam. Here's an idea: couldn't I come with you? I might be of use. I could help you solve all riddles, find all facts." There was an excited gleam in her eyes. "I am quite thorough."

"I am sure you are." Ezra imagined dissecting the heart with Loveday Finch peering over his shoulder. He backed away, holding the bag tight across his body. "But no, Miss, I do not need your help."

"Mr McAdam, are you afraid of me?" Loveday said.

Ezra thought of the men in the Fortune of War. "Absolutely not."

"Well then." She picked up her walking stick. "I have just had an idea – the very best. We should work together, as a team. I should have something to do and perhaps we might earn some money." She was grinning. Ezra tried to speak but failed. "We could discover truths and right wrongs."

"I don't think so, Miss Finch." He shook his head. "This is the stuff of children's play."

"No, I am quite serious. It would be perfect. Falcon and Finch may be no more, but Finch and McAdam are just beginning!"

Chapter Five

Mr William McAdam's Anatomy School and
Museum of Curiosities
Great Windmill Street
Soho
London
November 1792

The master had been called away to a private patient in the village of Hampstead and would have to stay over. Consequently Ezra had so much work to do that it wasn't until the following day that he could get a good look at the heart. Alone in the laboratory, he took the jar down off the shelf. He had added preserving fluid and the heart bobbed and floated in its jar like an oversized pickled walnut.

He was glad to be free of Miss Loveday Finch, her yellow house and her cracked ideas. He was not, and would not be, a part of some theatrical double act or wild thief-taking partnership. He imagined she must have read about such things in one of those ladies' novels, or perhaps because she worked on the stage her imagination was overly stimulated. Ezra sighed. The heart sat on the wooden table dead and cold. He moved the magnifying lens into place and reminded himself that he was doing this for two guineas and for his future. With Anna or not.

But he could not help becoming interested. What had caused these unnatural effects? It seemed undersized, as if it had been squeezed. He smelt it, touched it – the smell was not unusual but the texture and weight was. No wonder the man had died. How could this tiny shrivelled thing pump enough blood around a grown man's body? But what could have caused it? Some kind of disease? Some kind of drug?

Ezra took his scalpel and sliced the organ, as neatly as he could, in two. It fell open like some outlandish but rotten fruit, dark and already beginning to smell. The four chambers were clear enough; there was nothing obvious impeding its action – only its withered size and thickened walls.

Ezra sat back and pushed the lens out of the way. He took out his notebook to see if he had written anything down during the lecture, and that was when he came across the oblong of skin he had excised the night before last. He had forgotten all about it after everything that had happened – the attempted break-in, and Miss Loveday Finch.

Ezra retrieved it, sponged it and pinned it out on a flat wax-covered tray. He could see the mark clearly now, a definite letter in tattoo-ink blue, curved and swirling like a wave. The master would know where he could find an Arabic dictionary.

He needed help with the heart as well. Mr McAdam would know exactly what had happened to it, or at least point him on the correct path. The shelf above the desk groaned with books, rows and rows stretching up to the ceiling: anatomy, the mysteries of circulation, the weight of the brain. Any one of them might have the answer, but where to start?

Perhaps he should take a walk, clear his mind in the fresh air. That was, after all, one of the recommendations the master usually made. Ezra made a thorough sketch of the heart as it was now and pinned it up above the table next to a drawing of a healthy organ to remind him of the differences. Then he put the heart back into a jar, untied his laboratory apron and went downstairs. He would take a cup of coffee and walk as far as St James's Park. The cold frost might order his thoughts.

Ezra heard voices before he reached the kitchen – Mrs Boscaven was laughing. He pushed open the door … and there, in his own kitchen, sitting around the big fire taking coffee with Mrs Boscaven, Ellen and Toms as cosy as if she'd sat there a thousand times before, was Miss Loveday Finch producing a scarlet handkerchief from the sleeve of her mourning gown. No one bothered to look up as he entered; they were all transfixed, Ellen and Mrs B clapping, even Toms smiling and saying, "Well done, Miss!" as though he'd never seen a conjuring trick in his life.

"Miss Finch!" Ezra could not keep the surprise from his voice. "What are you doing here? I haven't had a chance to—"

"That's no way to greet lady callers," Toms said. "You'll have to excuse Ezra, Miss. He's no good around ladies – or the living in general."

"Pull up a chair, Ez," Mrs Boscaven said. "Poor Miss Finch has told us how as you're helping her with her father."

"Has she?" He looked at Loveday but she didn't meet his gaze. How much had she told them? Ezra found that telling the whole world one's business was never the best way forward.

"And she's been entertaining us all with tales of Mr Finch. You never mentioned Miss Finch, Ez," chastised Mrs Boscaven. "The master'll be proud of you, offering to help a young lady like that."

"Oh yes. I am indeed very grateful," said Miss Finch, smiling demurely. Ezra gave her a look.

He didn't remember her being grateful when he carried her into Bart's.

"Who'd have known what would have happened to my leg," she went on. She sipped her tea. "It's already much better – and, before you ask, Mr McAdam, yes, I have been using a stick."

"And she were conjuring," Ellen told him. "Doing tricks. Go on, make the hanky disappear again, Miss!"

"Conjuring? I thought you were in mourning," said Ezra. He went to find his special coffee cup but *she* was using it.

"Oh, don't be such a gowk!" Toms said. "It's not your father passed." He lowered his voice so only Ezra could hear and said, "As if you had one anyway."

Ezra ignored him, poured some coffee into another cup and drank it standing up.

"We had no idea you moved in theatrical circles, Ez. Miss Finch's life is so interesting. Did you know she and her poor father have lately returned from Vienna *and* Constantinople? And she has lived in Paris – before the revolution."

"A wonderful city, Mrs Boscaven," Miss Finch said. "Quite beautiful. When Pa and I performed at…" Her voice trailed off and she sniffed and dabbed at her eyes. Toms looked smitten. Ezra sipped his coffee. Was this the same girl who'd happily fought a whole inn of resurrection men?

Mrs Boscaven nodded. "But we've heard the French king has been arrested! Imagine that! I don't know what to think. Wasn't the master planning on taking you, Ez?"

"Yes, to the Hôtel-Dieu to see M. Desault," Ezra said. "Mr McAdam says that French surgeons are the very best."

"Perhaps when the revolution settles down…" Mrs Boscaven got up.

"I'm not sure that is what revolutions do, Mrs B." Ezra smiled.

"Well, I think the French king had it coming," Toms said, and reached out for a biscuit. Ezra said nothing. He didn't want to be seen to agree with Toms.

"I reckon as the whole world is in turmoil." Mrs Boscaven prodded at the fire. "The Russians and the Swedes."

"And the Ottomans," Toms added.

Ezra looked at him. "I didn't realize you were so interested in foreign news."

Toms gave him a filthy look. Ezra thought he saw Miss Finch smile behind her handkerchief.

"And we had cracksmen trying to smash into the house," Ellen said, a little bit scared.

"They didn't get in, Ellen. It was only a pair of rascals looking for easy pickings." Ezra tried to reassure her with a smile, but it was a poor smile. He had an idea that whoever those men had been they knew quite well whose house it was. And that they would be back.

"Oh, this world is a sad and terrible place," Mrs Boscaven said.

"Death – if you'll pardon me, Miss Finch – is all around us," commented Ezra.

"Never truer than in this house," Toms added. "Death is the old man's trade. All that cutting up, all them *things*, all those gory whatsits up in your museum."

"That's where you're wrong, Toms," Ezra told him. "It's not about death. Not at all."

"I don't think I'm wrong, am I, Miss Finch?" Toms smiled at her. "I mean to say, I don't suppose you hold with any of that business, nice girl like yourself?"

Miss Finch smiled back. "Of course not, Mr Toms. Naturally I despise resurrectionists and those who encourage them."

"Call me Henry," he said. Ezra rolled his eyes.

"But I see the value of science, of course." She looked at Ezra. "And now I am here, I would so love to see the museum."

Ezra drained his coffee cup and stood up. "I was just going out, as a matter of fact." He would not let her have it all her way.

Toms jumped up. "I don't mind showing you round, Miss."

"That's so kind of you." She paused; threw Ezra another look. "Henry."

Toms blushed. She was playing with him. Ezra almost felt sorry for the man.

"He doesn't know one end of the human body from another," Ezra said.

"I think," Toms retorted, "I know a good deal more about living bodies than ever you do."

"That is not what I meant."

"Boys!" Mrs Boscaven shook her head. "I think you should both escort Miss Finch around the museum." She looked hard at Toms. "You know how particular the master is about his objects. Although I warn you, Miss Finch, it is not for the fainthearted. And boys, if she so much as blanches, you bring her back down here, quick sharp. Is that clear?"

They answered together, like chastened schoolboys, "Yes, Mrs Boscaven."

"Mr McAdam's museum is spoken of all across town," Miss Finch said, following Toms and Ezra upstairs.

"He could make a deal of cash selling tickets," Toms muttered. "I would. I'd spend it on a matching pair of black prancers."

"Toms, this is not a side show," Ezra said, opening the door. "The museum is a tool for science. We are endeavouring to make the world a better place. To cure illness, to know how disease works."

"But mostly you cut up dead folk," Toms said, smirking. Ezra wished that he could knock the smile clear off Toms' face.

The low afternoon sun slanted into the room through floor-to-ceiling south-facing windows. On the far wall were shelf upon shelf of jars, each containing a specimen. The preserving fluid in which they floated shone like gold in the sunlight, like so much treasure. In the centre of the room stood three glass cases containing larger specimens.

"That's the Irish Giant," Toms said, pointing to the skeleton in the largest case.

Miss Finch gasped, but she was not looking at the skeleton. She had seen the child-sized shape made of veins and arteries. It was like a ghost child, or a human leaf skeleton: no bones, just blood vessels fanning out from the heart. After her initial shock, Ezra could see, Miss Finch was quite fascinated.

"It's a circulatory map," he explained.

"Are those real arteries?" she gasped. "From a real child?"

"I'm afraid so. We spent days heating and colouring the wax, feeding it through the blood vessels so that there could be an accurate representation of how blood flows."

"How on earth do you remove them from the body?" She took a step closer.

Ezra opened his mouth to explain.

"You don't want to know," Toms cut in. Ezra glared at the back of his head.

"But that is truly astounding!" Miss Finch shook her head, wide-eyed, and Ezra allowed himself a little smile.

"That's nothing," Toms told her. "You should see bone boy's tumour."

"Tumour?"

"Didn't he tell you?" Toms grinned. "Haven't you noticed that great scar down his mug?"

"Oh! I thought it was won at a duel or fight," Miss Finch

said. She looked at Ezra and his hand went up to the scar.

Toms laughed. "Him, with a sword! Tell me you never thought old bookworm Ezra here a fighter!"

Miss Finch flushed red.

Toms scanned the jars. "Here's old Ez's tumour, fresh as the day the master sliced it off."

The jar was a big one, almost a foot tall. Toms took it in two hands and presented it to her. Inside, floating in preserving fluid, was a large fleshy mass about eight inches long and four inches in circumference. Miss Finch's mouth had dropped open.

"Awful, isn't it? Must've been bigger than Ez's head. Although I don't think his looks have been much improved by its removal, eh, Miss Finch? The master bought him because he thought this lump made him interesting. How much did you cost, Ezra? Tuppence in Spanish Town? Or did the master get you free with a sugar loaf?"

Ezra took the jar from Loveday Finch and set it firmly back upon the shelf.

"You were a slave?" she asked him.

"Still is, officially, I reckon," Toms put in. "Rightly, I reckon as the master should sell him back to some sugar plantation."

"I am *not* a slave, Miss Finch. The master freed me, and you know that, Toms," Ezra snapped. "I am his apprentice. And you're an idiot, a fart catcher, a bully with fists instead of a brain."

"You hear that, Miss Finch?" Toms faced Ezra. He was taller by a few inches and broader in the shoulder. "I'll give you a slap if I have to."

"You don't dare!" Ezra didn't move away.

"Stop it!" Loveday Finch stepped between them. "I wish to look around this museum, not watch two idiots pick a squabble."

"I am not the idiot," Ezra muttered.

"Nor me," Toms added.

Miss Finch walked smartly away from them down the length of the room, taking time over the tapeworm coiled inside one jar and the stillborn baby attached to a placenta in another. She didn't shrink or show disgust at all. Ezra couldn't help but admire that.

"She's a cracker, that one, no mistake," Toms said to him, and Ezra swallowed, for he was thinking the exact same thought.

"You're making a fool of yourself, Toms." Ezra said it quietly so Miss Finch wouldn't hear. "She's not interested in you."

"And you think you have a chance with her, do you?" Toms said. "Can't stay true to your Anna for five minutes. What were you thinking when you were sewing up her leg, eh?"

Ezra felt the anger rising up again. "I am *not* interested in Miss Finch."

"Then let me have her," Toms whispered back.

"What's this?" Loveday Finch called from the far end of the room. She had pushed open the door to the laboratory. Toms ran after her, ready to help.

"It's the laboratory, Miss. Where they get stuff ready, I think." Ezra shook his head and followed. What had he ever done to deserve Toms?

"Mr McAdam! What is this? Where did you get this?" Loveday Finch's voice was raised.

Ezra ran down the length of the museum. Perhaps she had found the heart... But no, she wasn't looking at that. Not even at the drawing labelled FINCH, pinned up on the wall. She was examining the piece of skin with the tattoo.

"You know what it says? Is it Arabic?"

"Yes, absolutely. I have seen it before – well, I have seen people with this mark before," she went on. "At the Ottoman court in Constantinople."

"And?" Ezra asked. "Can you read it?"

She shook her head regretfully. "No, but whoever had this mark was of the harem, in the royal service."

"The harem, eh?" Toms said, interested.

Loveday Finch sat down and moved the magnifying lens across the piece of skin.

Toms peered over her shoulder at the skin and made a face.

"Look, Miss Finch," Ezra said, "I should like to talk to you about your father."

"Good." She was still looking at the skin. "Have you found something?"

Ezra paused. He looked at Toms. "Are you still here?"

"I am, and I think I could help Miss Finch a deal more than you when it comes to the mystery of her father's death!"

Ezra sighed. "Miss Finch, I think it is important that you don't go blabbing your business all around town."

"I do not!"

"See, bone boy, she does not." Toms leant against the table and faced Ezra, arms folded.

This was no good. "I'm going out," Ezra said. "Toms

can show you anything else you want to see." He turned to Toms and added, "Provided you put it back."

Toms grinned. "I'm more than happy, Miss Finch, to show you everything."

Ezra almost groaned out loud. He left them to it, fetched his good coat and his notebook and went out into the bone-cold blue-grey streets.

As he left the house Ezra barely took in the man leaning on the railings of Mrs Perino's. He saw him but dismissed him: he looked like a drover up from town in a sheepskin jacket and a pair of long boots. Ezra did not see the man empty his pipe onto the ground and follow him down to the cloth warehouse.

Ezra did not want to think of intrigue and murder and magicians; he wanted to talk to Anna. There was no response when he knocked on the door to the kitchen, and Ezra was about to give up and leave when it finally drew open and Betsey was there, hand to her lips.

"Don't you say a word, Ezra McAdam," she whispered. "If Mr David finds you he'll tan your hide and make a waistcoat out of you!"

"Don't worry, Betsey." He spoke softly too. "I just want to see Anna one last time, if you could take a message for me."

Betsey said nothing. She didn't move.

"Betsey, please! I'll get some more of that rubbing preparation for your joints – you said as it did you the world of good."

Betsey pulled the kitchen door closed behind her and stepped out into the mews, casting a quick wary look up at the house. "I can't, Ezra."

"For me, Betsey. For Anna."

Betsey sighed. "She's gone, isn't she. They packed her off to Holland like she told you."

"What? Already?" Ezra knew organs did not shift in the body, but he swore he felt his heart sink. "Is there an address? Can I write to her, Betsey?"

"Oh, Ez, lad. It's best you don't. You're only young. There'll be so many more girls, I swear, for a good-looking young man like yourself. Why, if I were ten years younger..."

Ezra couldn't smile.

There was the sound of a door slamming somewhere up in the St John house, and Betsey told him to get off home, out of the cold, before he froze.

Chapter Six

St Anne's Churchyard
Princes Street
London
November 1792

The clear sky had begun to cloud over; a few tiny dry flakes of snow drifted down. Ezra stuck his hands deep in his pockets. Perhaps he would not go as far as St James's Park. He went to the parish house and left a message about the break-in for the watch, and then to the churchyard of St Anne's, to the spot where he would often meet with Anna.

They would sit on the bench, a wooden plank hard against the west wall of the church, facing the gravestones lined up in rows waiting for the last trump. He brushed the snowflakes aside and sat down.

What would the end be like? Ezra wondered. Would the ground crack open? Would the dead rise up? How could that be when flesh rotted and even bones turned to ash eventually? He and Anna talked about this often; she was a literalist while he would argue that the Bible must be interpreted for the modern world. Ezra would have liked to talk to her now. About the tongueless cadaver and the break-in, as well as Mr Finch's heart. She would have an idea worth hearing even if he did not agree with it.

She would tell him, sharply and to the point, that he should leave the Finch girl and her silly ideas well alone. Even if the facts concerning the death of Mr Finch and the tongueless man seemed to have something in common, what could he do about any of it?

He stamped his feet and blew into his hands to keep warm. If he wanted to earn those two guineas, he had better have some ideas. He needed to know not just why the heart was so deformed, but – perhaps more importantly – if there was anyone who would benefit from Mr Charles Finch's sudden demise. He could only find that out by talking to the girl again, speaking to those her father worked with, perhaps going through his personal effects, the props they used for shows. Would Mr Falcon earn more working solo? Did Mrs Gurney have something to gain? He smiled to himself. The yellow paint in her drawing room might have been criminal, but he couldn't really see the landlady committing murder.

Ezra looked up and noticed a large man sharpening his knife against the stone wall of the graveyard, watching him. It was the same man he'd glimpsed outside the house, the one he'd thought a drover, tall and broad. Ezra frowned. Had the chap followed him? The man did not look away, and as he stared he spat onto the ground. There was something deeply unsettling about him, and it was not simply the way he held his knife, pausing to check the blade, running it between forefinger and thumb, all the while never taking his eyes from Ezra. There was also a fierce coldness about his eyes.

The snow became heavier. Ezra heard the man hawk up a great gobbet of phlegm and saw him aim it out across the graves in his direction. Ezra stood up. He would not be intimidated. The master always said it was better to ask a question than to wait and speculate unnecessarily.

"Hey!" he shouted. "You, sir! If you want something you would do as well to ask!"

The man looked behind him, slowly, as if he had all the time in the world. He didn't pocket the knife but kept hold of it, blade out, and walked towards him. Ezra swallowed. He looked around for a weapon – a stone, anything. If only he carried a scalpel! But he could not imagine using it on a living person, even the lumbering shape that approached through the snow, which was now falling more heavily.

"Ezra! Ezra McAdam!" He heard a voice calling him from the other side of the churchyard, over towards Rupert Street. A girl's voice – for a moment he imagined Anna come to tell him she was not travelling after all. But what about the rogue lumbering towards him with a knife?

"Anna!" He should warn her she needed to run.

He looked back towards the man. There was nobody there. No one at all. Even through the blur of snowflakes he could tell the drover had gone. He leant against the wall of the church, his heart pounding ten to the dozen. Had he really been so scared? Not for himself, of course.

"Anna! Where are you?"

"Anna? I am not Anna!" Miss Finch was everywhere. "I have been all over, around Leicester Square and back along Lisle Street – Mr Toms said— Are you quite well?"

"Yes, of course." Ezra straightened up, shrugged the

snow off his jacket. He did not want Miss Finch to see how scared he had been. "Please do not tell me what Mr Toms said. I have had quite enough of him for one day."

Miss Finch wore a black fur hat. Snowflakes attached themselves to it and she shook them off.

"I ought to apologize," she said, "for turning up unannounced."

"It is done," Ezra said, tipping his cap at her. "I am on my way home." He looked around again – there was no sign of the man.

"No! Mr McAdam, I do need to talk to you, and you are right, I did not want your Mr Toms to know everything." She sighed. "I had to get out. Mrs Gurney's house is so quiet. It is all ticking-clock silence, and now that Pa is in the front parlour in his box it is only worse. It seems to have unsettled Mrs Gurney no end. She stalks the house like a spooked cat."

"I am sorry for you. But the weather is turning, I should get home – as should you."

"I wanted to say thank you, for finding Pa."

"Well, that was what you engaged me for."

"I know, and I am grateful." She put her hand on Ezra's arm and smiled. "Honestly I am."

"Do not flutter your eyelashes at me, Miss Finch. I am a different kettle of fish from Mr Toms."

Miss Finch was indignant. "I was *not* fluttering my eyelashes at Mr Toms. I was merely interested in the museum. And I am not fluttering them at you!"

"You could lower your voice, Miss Finch."

"I would remind you I am your employer! I take it you still want to earn your two guineas?"

"I do," Ezra said. He should not let irritation get in the way of his investigation.

"Well then," Miss Finch said. "I wish to talk with you. Now."

Ezra led her towards a tea shop in Panton Square. Inside, there was a good fire, and the windows were fogged with condensation. Ezra ordered hot chocolate and they sat down.

"Miss Finch," he began, "when I saw your father's body, it was clear someone had already…"

"Already what?"

Ezra shifted in his seat. "Taken something. Taken parts out of his body – namely, the stomach. I think whoever did it was trying to conceal proof of poisoning."

Loveday Finch sat back, satisfied. "There. I knew it."

"Please, there is a long way to go before we reach any conclusion." He took out his notebook. "I need to know if anyone hated your father, or wanted him dead. Perhaps I could speak with Mr Falcon?"

She almost laughed. "Mr Edward Falcon would never have killed Pa. He is bereft! He has had to change the act all about." She shook her head. "It has caused him far too much trouble."

Ezra sipped his chocolate. "Still, it would be most useful if you could arrange a meeting. So I can see for myself."

"I will, although I do not think it will lead to anything. He is so desperate he has asked me to perform. But I am still in mourning."

"I should have thought that would pose you no problem," Ezra said.

"I would not do it," she said. "Mrs Gurney would

throw me out." She was quiet a moment. "But I am sure Pa would not mind; performing is our livelihood. In one way or another. And I have been doing our accounts. Pa said we would be living high off the hog once we returned from Constantinople, but I suppose he had not reckoned on his own death." Miss Finch sighed and Ezra felt uncomfortable thinking about his payment.

"Oh, I can see what you are thinking. Your two guineas are safe. My father has provided me enough." Miss Finch shrugged. "I can stay at Mrs Gurney's as long as I wish. She has been kind, in her own way."

Ezra could see from her face that Miss Finch did not regard an indefinite stay at Mrs Gurney's to be the perfect legacy. However, she was not one to dwell on the unknown. She shook back her red curls, took a piece of paper out of her bag and began to unfold it. "Take a look at this. I thought it might be interesting." She slid the paper across the table. "Mr Falcon has another performance at the embassy, a seasonal reception, it says, three weeks from now."

"At the same address as before?" Ezra sat up. "It might be useful. Are you sure there is no party at the embassy who would gain from your father's death?"

"No, of course not. We are – were – entertainers. I admit the politics of the Ottoman court can be extreme, but we were never a part of all that. I cannot imagine there is anything anyone would have achieved by his death."

"Well, it could help to see where your father last worked – if you could perhaps get me admittance?"

"I am sure I could." Miss Finch leant towards him. "And I was thinking about something else I could help with, or that someone at the embassy could, at least."

Ezra frowned.

She laughed. "My goodness, for one supposedly so skilful with a knife you can be rather slow! Your sign, the tattoo on that piece of skin. They would know all about it there. Discovering its meaning would be simply done."

Ezra wondered. It was bound to be dangerous, seeking the man a cadaver had been. It might cause all sorts of problems for the master. But the honey cakes, they were Eastern too, weren't they? Perhaps both men were caught in the same web. "You think our cadaver worked at the embassy too?"

"Not if he was in the harem, as we suspect. The harem never travel. It is a kind of prison. A luxurious one, but a prison all the same."

"Do not expect me to feel sorry for royalty," Ezra said. "They take the lion's share of everything and are happy to let the poor starve."

"Don't you ever listen? The sultan's wives never leave the palace. And it is worst of all for any sons they may have. There is so much intrigue and plotting that the eldest sons of the sultan live closely confined until the sultan dies. One was locked up for so long he went mad!"

"There, you see. Such wealth and power only lead to corruption."

"No one deserves to suffer," Loveday protested. "Rich or poor."

Ezra humphed. "In my observation," he said, "the rich usually manage to avoid their share of suffering. You should see the scraps and destitutes we get at Mr McAdam's Monday clinics. I am sure every one of them would love to suffer as the rich do."

"Ezra McAdam, you are quite the revolutionary! Perhaps you would prefer to work for more equitable a fee? One guinea, perhaps? Ten shillings?"

"That is not what I meant!"

Loveday Finch made a face.

"Do not tease me, Miss Finch. I am of the belief that life should be fairer. In every way."

"You would change the world, then?"

"They have done it in France, in America…"

Miss Finch sipped her chocolate. "Perhaps. But I at the moment only want to find out who would make me an orphan. And I would put money on there being some connection between my father's death and this cadaver. You are an intelligent young man, Ezra McAdam. Don't you want to know the man's story?"

"No." Ezra said it firmly – too firmly, perhaps.

"I can tell that you do. You are just as intrigued as I."

"Maybe. But if it was known that a cadaver of the embassy household ended up on the master's anatomy table, it could be dangerous – and besides, there is no proof to link his death with that of your father."

"Yet!" Miss Finch's sea-grey eyes glowed. "I cannot resist a good mystery."

Ezra looked around the tea rooms. "Promise me, please, Miss Finch, do not mention this to a living soul."

"Who do you take me for?" She was affronted.

"I take you for one whose lips are far too loose for my liking."

She ignored this slight. "I could help, don't you see?"

"I said I have no interest in the business."

"You are a poor liar, Mr McAdam, and I am a professional one."

Ezra knew the master could get in a deal of trouble if the cadaver could be traced to them, and he resolved to be rid of the skin specimen as soon as he got home. "Miss Finch," he said, "I am trying to solve the riddle of your father's death. That is what you engaged me for. You should not have seen that tattoo, and I would prefer it if you could bring yourself to think you had not."

"How curious, you look quite perturbed by the matter."

"I assure you I am not," Ezra said shortly. He stood up. "I would like to speak to Mr Falcon as soon as can be arranged."

"If you wish, I will send word to you tomorrow."

"And you should take a cab back to Clerkenwell," Ezra added. "Your leg needs rest even if you do not."

Ezra walked home quickly. He went straight upstairs and unpinned the square of skin from its wax bed. He would get rid of it now, before he changed his mind – before Miss Finch's proposition started to seem too tempting. He took it out to the anatomy room, lit and stoked up the brazier, and tossed it in. He regretted it at once. The room filled with a smell not unlike the hog roast at a fair. The skin crackled and hissed for what seemed an age considering its tiny size.

Anna would have told him off; she would have imagined the cadaver answering the judgement trump with a square of skin missing. But Anna was not here. Ezra knew the cadaver would have a rather nasty scar up his chest, too. But he had more than likely been a Turk, and Ezra had no idea if they had a heaven or a hell or something else entirely. In any case, who knew where his tongue had got to? Lying bleeding on the floor of some tiled Ottoman palace, or perhaps on the sand in some vast hot desert.

When the ashes had cooled Ezra raked them out and went to the yard to empty them into the rubbish heap. Suddenly, he was aware of someone watching. There, by the street entrance, was a boy of nine or ten, wearing a cap that looked too big, a filthy jacket and old boots. He was pale-skinned and dark-eyed, and a lick of hair as dark as a raven's wing flopped out of his cap and across his face. The boy nodded at him, looked back into the street, then crossed the yard. Ezra wondered what he was after, bread or ashes by the looks of him.

"I say!" The boy spoke with the confidence and authority of money. "Young man."

Ezra looked back. "Are you addressing me?"

"I am. Are you Mr McAdam's black?" The boy's voice sounded strange – good fine English but odd, deep vowels. Though he seemed nervous, as if he expected a hand to reach out from Great Windmill Street and grab him at any moment.

"That is one way of putting it." Ezra folded his arms. This boy was a rum fish. His voice and bearing were one thing, his clothes another entirely.

"Can I speak with the man, your master? Now."

"He is not here. But with your manners, I doubt I would have let you in anyway," Ezra retorted.

"This is most urgent." Now the boy was closer Ezra could see there was a fierce anxiety in him, and he was pale with cold. Ezra shouldn't have been so hard on him. He bent down, his face level with the boy's.

"I am sorry, but he's away from home." The boy's face fell. Ezra softened. "Perhaps I can help. I could fetch you tea in the kitchen if you would like?"

"No, I cannot stay. You are anatomists, yes?"

Ezra nodded.

"You have bodies, a deal of dead bodies for your students."

He nodded again.

"I am looking for another black, a man, taller than you – he may have been shot."

Ezra was afraid his face betrayed him.

"Yes! You have seen him! I can tell! Is he still here? Did you see a letter in his jacket, or about his person?"

"When we see them," Ezra said gently, "they are not generally dressed."

The boy almost deflated.

"Please. Come in and have some tea." Ezra put a hand out to the boy's shoulder.

"Don't you dare touch me!" The boy's dark eyes were furious, scared, and he shrugged off Ezra's hand and ran. Ezra followed him, through the arch and up towards Soho Square.

As he turned into Dean Street Ezra slipped on some ice and landed heavily on his backside. By the time he stood up, winded and aching, the boy had completely vanished. The city, he reminded himself, was full of such poor souls, thousands of them. Perhaps when he had his own practice he would run free surgeries two days a week, or even three.

Ezra walked back home lost in thought. The mystery deepened. Who was he? That boy could pass for Turkish – had he been thrown out of the embassy, cast aside for making a mistake? Perhaps he had seen something pertaining to Mr Finch's death? Why hadn't Ezra thought to ask his name when he had the chance? He had thought that cadaver was too unusual, that someone like that would be missed! What would the master make of it? he wondered. If only he was here.

Ezra climbed up to the museum and went to close the curtain. The snow was still falling; the master would not be home this evening. Ezra could see down into the front drawing room of Mrs Perino's house where the fire blazed, and out across the city. The cloth warehouse was so near, yet Anna St John may as well have left for the Continent already.

Something caught his eye in the street, the flash of a pipe being lit. He looked down. The man he had seen in St Anne's churchyard was now standing across the road, leaning on Mrs Perino's railings, watching the front of the house. Ezra shivered and quickly pulled the curtains shut.

Toms had gone home. He was alone in the house with Mrs Boscaven and Ellen. What should he do? What if a party of cracksmen came in the night? Ezra went around the whole house, checked all the locks back and front. He slid the bolts on the front area door and went to the master's laboratory to check the bolts on the window. When he looked through the crack in the shutters he saw that the man had gone.

There was something distinctly unsettling about the

man, he thought: unsettling and suspicious. One more puzzle that a conversation with the master would set to rights. Ezra sat down at the table in the laboratory, lit a couple of candles and took down some books concerning circulation and the workings of the heart. Mr Finch should be his priority.

But the words and pictures swam in front of his eyes. He could not concentrate. Was that fellow outside one of the coves he had heard outside the anatomy room? Perhaps he was with the boy? And the cadaver with the tattoo, who had he been? Was Miss Finch correct? Was he really a member of the Ottoman household? If he was, who was the strange boy, and was he a foreigner too? Why in heaven's name had the man been shot in the back? Why wasn't it all over the newspapers? And why couldn't Ezra forget? After all, there had been so many – what was one tongueless man among an army of dead?

Chapter Seven

Mr William McAdam's Anatomy School and
Museum of Curiosities
Great Windmill Street
Soho
London
November 1792

It was late. Outside the snow had stopped falling at last, but not soon enough – Mr McAdam had been forced to remain another night in Hampstead, and Ezra was alone.

He was still working in the laboratory adjoining the museum when he was startled by the rumble of a cart turning into the yard. For a second Ezra froze, imagining an army of cracksmen ready to break the glass of the anatomy room and pour into the house. But when he looked out of the back window he recognized Mr Allen's cart. By the time Ezra had run down the stairs and drawn the bolts on the lecture room door, the man was waiting. It felt as though the thaw was in the air, but the ground was still white, which made the evening strangely bright.

Mr Allen's boy had jumped down too, and Ezra watched as he began to push a large wickerwork hamper off the back of the cart.

"No!" Ezra called. "We don't need a delivery. I thought Mr McAdam had sent word."

Allen waved at the boy, who shrugged and pushed the hamper back.

"No, he never did." Allen sniffed. "Well, I need a word now I'm here," he said quietly. "With the old man."

"The lecture tomorrow morning's off. The master's stuck up in Hampstead with the weather," Ezra told him, watching the clouds of hot, wet air rise up off the pony's neck.

"Is that so?" Something about the way the man spoke made Ezra wish he'd kept his own mouth firmly shut. "Shame."

"I'm sure he'll be back soon now the weather's changed. And if it's anything urgent…"

Allen shifted and looked around as if he expected somebody to be watching. He leant close. Ezra could smell liquor on his breath, and dirt that seemed to have penetrated the man's skin.

"There's been a problem," Allen said, "with one of your recent deliveries."

"What kind of problem?" Though Ezra reckoned he knew exactly where the problem lay.

"Someone's been asking questions. Seems the foreign one was some important cove."

"The cadaver without a tongue." Ezra said it aloud, without thinking.

"Don't ask me. We never look in their mouths." Allen's tone was suddenly icy. "Unless the teeth are good and we know someone who needs a set." He shuffled closer. "Just remember, if anyone does start poking around asking stuff, you never got it from us. See." He jabbed a grimy gloved finger in Ezra's chest and stared, his eyes as cold as two balls of dirty snow. "You don't even know my name."

Ezra stared back and answered coolly, "I am not scared of you, Allen."

At that moment the boy called down from the cart. "Pa, shall we take this one to St Thomas's, then?"

Mr Allen snarled at him. "How many times? I ain't your pa!"

The boy flinched. Allen swore, hawked up a ball of phlegm and spat onto the snow. Like the drover, Ezra thought.

"I'm training him up." Allen smiled, his teeth were like gravestones. "Just like your boss is training you."

It wasn't worth saying anything. Ezra wished the man would just go. "We'll see you next week, then," he said. "As usual."

"God willing." Allen waved and climbed up onto the cart. "If you lot have one, that is." Ezra watched as he flapped the reins against the pony's back and the cart rolled away into the night.

Ezra followed the cart out into the quiet, snow-muffled street and shivered. The man was unpleasant, he told himself. Nothing more. But someone else was clearly looking for the cadaver – well, for the man the cadaver had been. *Who*, though? The strange cove he'd seen watching the house and in the churchyard? And was there any connection between him and the boy with the bearing that said money and the smell that did not? Ezra looked up and down Great Windmill Street but it was empty. All folk, honest or black-hearted, were at home by their fires, and that lifted his spirits a little.

There was a symphony of drips from the guttering of the house opposite, the thaw. London would soon be filthy and noisy again and the master would be home. All would be well.

Ezra stepped inside, drew the bolts again, all of them, and went upstairs.

The fire was still burning in the laboratory but it was bitter. He shivered again. That the human body could endeavour to keep warm when all around it the cold made death ever closer was indeed fascinating. How cold, he wondered, would a heart have to be before it ceased pumping? Ezra swore the master would know precisely, and he looked forward to being able to ask him about it over one of Mrs B's hot stews.

Ezra sat down at the bench and flicked through his notes on poisons. There were so many! He had found a number of toxins that could take effect in the twelve or so hours that had taken Mr Finch from sickness to death: digitalis, some West African plants, oleander and milk-weed, and quite a few more. They all affected the heart, or so it said in the master's books. But would any shrivel a man's heart *so* completely?

At least he could write to Miss Finch and say honestly that her father's death was unnatural. And that poison was the cause, he was sure. But how could he go about finding the reason, and who in heaven's name was the perpetrator? How was it to be discovered? All of the possible poisons needed to have been adminis-tered within the previous eighteen hours. It could only be Mrs Gurney, Mr Falcon or someone at the perform-ance the night before his death. And from Miss Finch's description there had been an audience of close to one hundred souls at the embassy that night. If he could find a motive... Ezra rubbed his eyes.

It was several days now since the man's death, and every moment that passed would, he reasoned, make it harder to find the culprit. He paced the length of the museum in the dark, the pinpricks of candlelight bounc-ing off every glass surface, but his mind was stuck.

It was no use, he would have to sleep on it. Ezra pinched the candle out and went to bed. Eventually he slept, deeply, and in his dreams he imagined him-self on stage in some kind of magic show. He was at the Ottoman Embassy; the audience were row upon row of tongueless, slit-eared men, arms folded, gunshot wounds weeping blood, silent and staring. Ezra was alarmed fur-ther to find the magician was not Mr Falcon but the master. Suddenly, with a wave of his wand, the master vanished, and Ezra was left alone, staring out into the crowd as they shuffled silently towards him.

He woke suddenly, his heart racing. His body was damp with sweat and he realized he was gripping the sheets. What on earth could it mean? He almost laughed at his own folly. Exactly nothing! He was entirely and completely rational. Interpreting dreams was for old women and country idiots.

There was a scraping and he sat bolt upright, but it was only Ellen. She was sweeping out the grate and laying the new fire in the soft dark of the early morning.

"Oh, I am sorry, Ez! I never meant to wake you."

"I was dreaming, Ellen. And you've done me a favour waking me. I'm thoroughly glad to be out of it."

Ellen lit the fire and stood up. "Thaw's come on, thank God. Master'll be home sometime today."

Ezra pulled the curtain back. There were some lamps lit in the houses opposite, and the sky was a curtain of light cloud. In the streets, the sound of the city waking up – iron wheels, horses' hooves, carts and trolleys and the *drip, drip* of melting snow – promised a return to normality. Ezra smiled.

He wrote to Miss Finch outlining his thoughts. He would confirm his thesis – that it was poison – as soon as the master returned. The cause, he wrote, and the perpetrator, sadly remained a mystery until he could discover a motive, which would take time. He dipped his pen into his inkwell and paused for a moment. Then he began writing again. It would further his work if he could make a visit to the embassy as soon as possible so that he could talk to all the relevant parties. Perhaps she would be so kind as to arrange it. He could not think of any other way.

He sealed the envelope with the master's wax and set it up ready to post.

One day he would be a surgeon and have his own place with a brass nameplate fixed to the wall. Anna's family might well look at him differently then. Perhaps Ellen would come and work for him as housekeeper, and he would leave Toms far behind, and good riddance. He would take a house in the newer developments north of Oxford Street, perhaps, where there was a little more space, and he would meet Mr McAdam as an equal at the Company of Surgeons dinners.

He got up, invigorated with the thought of a future that didn't include Toms, mystery cadavers and rash, impetuous, red-headed girls.

Today, Ezra decided, he would clean and sort the museum. He would shine the jars and order their display anew. It would act as an apology for being such an idiot and wanting to leave. It would show Mr McAdam that he was truly grateful – for his training, for his education and for his home – and it would set his own mind at ease to occupy himself with something familiar and certain. He set to work. He would be a credit to the master in every way.

Ezra worked without break, dusting, cleaning and writing new labels in his best hand for those that had faded. It was hard work but fulfilling: Ezra enjoyed being in the museum and there was a simple pleasure in the quiet, careful organization. When Mrs Boscaven came up with a tray of food as the clock at St Anne's struck three, he realized it had hardly occurred to him he was hungry.

"You'll waste away with no lunch," she said, setting the tray down. "There's some cold cuts and the end of the loaf. As it's quiet, Ellen and I are off to see the new Indian cottons in the Piccadilly warehouse before the dark comes down and supper needs cooking."

"Thank you, Mrs B." Ezra stretched and stepped down off the chair he'd been using to dust the top shelf.

Mrs Boscaven set her hands on her hips and looked round. "Well, well, you've done wonders in here. Though I don't like to look too closely at whatever it is you and the master keep in all these infernal jars."

Ezra smiled. "They're not infernal, Mrs B, honestly."

He lit the candles and went to close the curtains.

"Well, here's to hoping the master's travelled as far as Islington by now," Mrs Boscaven said. "With luck, he'll be home for supper. The street's almost back to its usual self. I heard a body crying for fresh fruit! Can't imagine what they meant in this weather – last summer's apples, I expect."

Ezra took the plate with the cold meat and bread, and tucked in. He was hungrier than he thought.

"How you can eat with all this stuff around, and the smell, heaven knows! I'd better send Toms out for some good cheese before the master gets in." Mrs Boscaven clucked away downstairs.

By the time Ezra heard the front door close, he'd finished his lunch and was onto his second cup of tea. He looked around, tired but satisfied. The museum had been transformed – the glass gleamed, the freshly penned labels stood out neat and clear. If only the puzzles of life were as easy to order as so many jars on shelves.

Ezra put the cup and plate back on the tray and took it downstairs to the kitchen. He helped himself to another couple of slices of cold ham and some of Mrs Boscaven's chutney. The kitchen windows were below street level and he could see it was already dark outside. But plenty of carts and wagons trundled past, and Ezra hoped Mrs B was right and that the master would be home for supper.

It was as he sat by the kitchen fire boiling the kettle for a third cup of tea that he heard a different sound. Not the shouts or the rumble of traffic from the street, it was the sound of breaking glass. And it came from above, from somewhere up in the house.

Ezra stood up, his heart jumping in his chest. He picked up the poker from where it leant against the fireplace. Should he shout? Would his mere presence be enough to scare a cracksman off? He gripped the poker tight.

He could hear a heavy tread. It sounded as if more than one person was up there. Ezra climbed the stairs from the basement to the ground floor – they were up in the museum. He took a deep breath and went up another flight.

For a moment he stood silently on the landing, holding the poker in both hands, listening. More breaking glass – and if he wasn't mistaken, that was the sound of a jar dropping. One of the jars from the most precious anatomical collection in London – possibly the world. All his work today, all the cleaning, all the sorting…

Ezra could not bring himself to be cautious any longer. He pushed open the door to the museum and swung wildly with the poker.

"Mr Ezra McAdam. Oh, please, put it away for God's sake." A thin man stood leaning against the mantelpiece. He was dressed in a fine wool jacket, expensive, pale grey, with a modern tall hat covering his hair, his skin a few shades lighter than Ezra's own. The man wore a small neat pointed beard, greying in places, and would not have looked out of place in one of the smarter arcades in Mayfair.

"Meet my friend Oleg," the man said. "You may have seen him … around."

Ezra turned. Standing in front of the broken first-floor window was the man he'd thought was a drover, wrapped in his sheepskin. He was holding a jar – the double-skulled foetus, a rare specimen that any surgeon would have been lucky to witness, never mind acquire perfectly preserved.

Ezra balked as it slipped through the man's fingers and smashed on the floor sending up a spray of foul-smelling embalming fluid.

"Oops," the man said. "Do be more careful, Oleg."

Ezra tried to make out his accent. Was it Turkish?

Oleg grinned and went to pick up another jar. Ezra swung the poker against his arm but the man brushed it away as if the iron rod smashing into his bone was no more than the flutter of a moth's wings.

Ezra hit again. Oleg moved slowly, looked at his arm then at Ezra. His eyes narrowed very slightly but otherwise he didn't even flinch.

The thin man had pulled something from his jacket. Ezra heard the snap and clack of a catch engaging. Very slowly, he turned to look.

The pistol was aimed at his heart.

He dropped the poker and watched it roll away under the cabinet of hands and feet.

Oleg suddenly swept his arm along the first row of jars, breaking ten, fifteen at once.

"No!" Ezra jerked forward, for a moment forgetting the gun.

"I wouldn't do that if I were you." The man had pulled the trigger back. Ezra put his hands up and retreated again, powerless to do anything but watch as years of work, hour upon hour of study, smashed and broke on the floor.

"Please! No more!" Ezra tried to keep his voice level but he could have wept; he could see the specimens all over the Turkish runner, formless like so many beached jellyfish, the liquid seeping away through the carpet and down between the floorboards.

"Now now, young Mr McAdam, there's still plenty more jars left for Oleg to break, and there's always your bones, too. I'm sure that he would oblige."

"With pleasure, Mr—" Oleg coughed, his voice was thicker, deeper – also foreign, but not Turkish. He nodded at the smarter man. "Mr Ahmat."

Ezra breathed deeply, trying to stay calm. The cold and rain were blowing in through the broken window, water spotting the books on the higher shelves.

"What is it you want?" he asked. "Anything. Take it and get out – the Irish Giant? Take it!" If only he could make them leave.

"In good time, boy," Mr Ahmat said coldly. Ezra watched as he removed his hat, bent down and lit his pipe with a taper lit from the fire. "And I think you know what we want. Clever boy like you. Apprentice surgeon, I heard. Not bad for a black, don't you reckon, Oleg?" Mr Ahmat smiled. It was the smile of a lipless man, flat and thin, showing teeth.

Oleg shrugged, his big hand reaching for another jar. Ezra tried not to look; he didn't want to know what it was.

"It's the tongueless cadaver, isn't it?" he said. The man was impassive. "The tongueless corpse. It's all about the bloody corpse. I knew it would bring trouble—"

"Corp*ses*," the man said, taking a pull on his clay pipe. "There were two."

Ezra frowned. "No, there was one – one man, a Negro, without a tongue – that's what you're talking about, and he's dead. You smashing this place up won't change that!"

"Corp*ses*," the man said again.

Ezra tried to think. What did he mean? "We see many, many corpses. Every week…"

"But there were two at the last lecture. My sources aren't wrong."

"Yes, there were two."

"See? That was not hard. And was there anything else? Any jewellery?"

"Of course not!" Ezra exclaimed. "No clothes, no jewellery, nothing. By the time they come to us we're lucky if they have their teeth. You must know that!" He looked from one man to the other. "They're bodies, cold meat. Things. No one bothers with them."

"That's where you're wrong," the man said. "We know there was a boy. And the boy had something we need. Some rubies."

"How? He had nothing!" Ezra could not think for the life of him why these men would have any interest in some workhouse boy with rickets; they were almost two a penny. "He had drowned."

"Drowned?" The gunman was suddenly interested. He looked across to Oleg. Oleg raised his eyebrows.

"You're sure?" The man's voice was clear and knife-sharp. Definitely foreign. Eastern, he was certain of it.

"Yes," Ezra replied. He was trembling, but the hand that held the gun, still pointing straight at him, was as steady as a rock. Ezra wondered if it was the same piece that had shot the tongueless man fatally in the back. One shot, that's all it would take, and he'd be bleeding out on the runner, slap-bang in the middle of the museum. He'd be snuffed out; finished. Ezra swallowed.

"Did you cut the boy open?" Mr Ahmat asked.

"Of course." Why weren't they interested in the Negro?

"Show me," said Ahmat. "Show me the body."

Ezra shook his head. "We don't keep the things here."

Mr Ahmat looked around at the jars lining the room. "It seems to me that you do."

"The remains are long gone." Ezra noticed the briefest flicker of regret on the man's face. He didn't think he'd be happy with one remaining thigh bone. "The cadavers are removed after the lectures," he continued. "It's probably three foot down in the St Pancras boneyard, or St Giles's – sometimes they use St Giles."

"Did you open him up?" The man was getting agitated. "Right up?"

"Stem to stern." Ezra drew a line from his collarbone to his stomach.

"Was there anything … anything odd? Describe him. Paint me a picture."

"There was nothing I'd not seen before." Ezra struggled to find words. "He'd have been nine, ten, hard to tell, he'd been in the water—"

"Could you tell how long, just from looking at him?"

"If I had my notebook. It's over there, in the laboratory."

Mr Ahmat nodded but kept his gun trained on Ezra as he fetched his book. Ezra made a show of looking for it, his mind racing all the while, wondering what he could do – if there was a way of disarming the gunman, getting hold of the gun, of dodging the man mountain that was Oleg and escaping to call the watch.

Mrs Boscaven and Ellen would be back soon; they might get hurt. He had to do something. Shout out of the window, yell for help?

There was a dissecting knife on the laboratory bench. It might be his only hope. With a quick glance at Mr Ahmat, Ezra palmed the blade and tucked it up his sleeve. Neither Ahmat nor Oleg seemed to have noticed. He could feel the cold metal hard against his skin as he walked back.

"Give it here." The man waved the gun again. Ezra passed the notebook over.

This was his chance. As Ahmat took the book from him Ezra lunged and stuck the knife into the soft flesh of his forearm. Ezra jumped back, the knife still in his hand. Blood gushed from the man's arm and the gun fell to the floor. Ahmat's eyes were flashing fury.

"Oleg!" he yelled.

Ezra felt Oleg jump him before he could even look round; he fell into the cabinet with the skeleton of the Irish Giant, glass, wood and bone splintering everywhere.

Ahmat held his bleeding hand. The curses that flew from his mouth weren't English.

Ezra tried to get up but was stopped by a sharp pain in his back. He swore under his breath. Above him, Oleg lifted a heavy boot and slammed it down towards his face. Ezra hardly had time to think. He took a piece of glass in his hand, twisted away from the boot just in time and plunged the glass through thick fabric into the flesh of his calf. Oleg screamed.

The gun lay on the floor. Ezra couldn't reach it; it was too far away. But he could get to the door. Get away.

He tried to stand up but the pain in his back was growing so he crawled, pulling himself inch by inch towards the door.

There was the crack of a gunshot. The ball whistled so close to his face he could feel the heat of it on his cheek. It thudded into the door, wood splintering. The smell of gunpowder and burnt wood joined the reek of blood and preserving fluid.

Ezra looked back. Mr Ahmat had picked up the pistol and he sat up, grey coat stained with red blood. He was swearing at Oleg – Ezra didn't understand the language but he knew curses when he heard them. He had to get up, had to run.

Ahead of him the door flew open. "Ezra! My God!" The master stood in the doorway holding a broom handle, taking in the scene with a look of horror, the floor awash with fluid and sparkling with a thousand shards of broken glass.

Ahmat and Oleg struggled to stand.

"Get out of my house! This instant!" Mr McAdam yelled, putting out a hand to Ezra and pulling him up.

"Get back, sir," Ezra shouted, "get back! There is a pistol!"

"The damned man wouldn't dare—"

At that moment the gun exploded again. Ezra watched the master step in front of him then falter and fall, like a felled tree, onto the soaked carpet. He saw his face register confusion, anger, then pain.

"Master!"

Oleg dragged himself to the open window and jumped. Ezra took the broom handle the master had dropped, but the gunman had stepped over him and was out of the room and down the stairs. Ezra heard another shot, and Toms shouting; then whistles in the street and cries for the watch.

Ezra turned back to Mr McAdam. He was face down, eye to eye with the double-skulled foetus.

"Ezra, lad," he said, and his eyes began to flutter shut.

"Keep still, sir. It will be all right."

"I am going, Ez."

"No, sir. It's a graze, surely!" Ezra cried and rolled him over. Blood blossomed on his master's shirt, the deep crimson stain spreading outward against the white linen. Ezra tore it open, the damp fabric shredding easily, and tried not to think of the wound in the chest of the tongue-less man.

"I'll get the ball out, sir," he sniffed, "and you'll be as right as rain. No doubt, sir."

"It's too late…"

"I'll not hear of it. No, sir!" Ezra insisted, but he could feel the tears prickling behind his eyes. He was being a fool; there was no cause for distress. Of course he would save him. The master had taught him everything he knew – what good had all that instruction been if he could not save him now?

Ezra took off his own jacket to use that to stop the bleeding, but even in the surgeries at Bart's he had never seen so much blood; he could not keep his hands from fumbling.

"I can stop it, sir, don't you worry. Compression will staunch the blood flow…"

The master put out his hand and took one of Ezra's. His grip was firm. That was a good sign.

"There, you will be all right," Ezra said, and sniffed again. "I am sorry about everything," he added. "Everything. I was never grateful enough." It was difficult to see, his eyes seemed to be somehow blurry.

"Ez, lad, shush." The master's voice was low. "Don't you fret."

Suddenly Mr McAdam's grip failed and his arm fell limp in Ezra's grasp. There was a noise from his throat, a kind of gurgling, coughing sound. Ezra had heard it before – it was the sound of the soul leaving the body. The death rattle.

The master had gone.

Chapter Eight

The Burial Ground of St George the Martyr
Bloomsbury
London
November 1792

On the morning of the funeral Ezra swept the anatomy room as usual, although he had no idea if the place would ever be in use again. But he had to keep busy, do something, anything so as not to think. He almost smiled. Wasn't that what Miss Finch had said?

When he opened the door into the yard he saw a girl wearing a travelling cloak, her pale face solemn.

"Anna! I thought you had gone!"

"Tomorrow," she said. Her eyes were red. "They do not know I am here, but when I heard about Mr McAdam... I was so sorry to hear of it. I could not leave without seeing you. I could not!"

"Don't cry, please." Ezra blinked. He could not bear this. "Will you write?"

"I will try. You know David."

Ezra threw the broom down onto the floor. "This is not right! This is not how it should be, the master dead and you going away!"

"Ezra, we cannot change this."

Ezra shrugged. "Who knows, I may be a free agent. I could travel anywhere, do whatever I want, now the master…"

Anna smiled. "Mr McAdam will look after you even in death. I do not doubt it."

"I could follow you, Anna, when things are settled."

"I must go. David is expecting me back," she said. She took something from inside her cloak. "This is yours, the book you lent me." It was the Tom Paine. "You never did quite rationalize me." She suddenly stepped towards him and threw her arms around his neck. Ezra had never felt her so close, warm and alive, and he hugged her back, tighter. He wanted to shout at her to tell her not to go, to stay with him and … and what? He didn't know his own future, how could he promise her anything at all? He pulled away, his eyes stinging, smarting.

"Goodbye, Ezra," she said, and slipped away into the street.

Ezra looked up at the heavy grey sky and the rain broke, cold, fat drops that ran down his face. He wiped them away. He had to be strong.

The rain had turned the graveyard into a sea of mud. Ezra looked down into the earth at the coffin and wished a thousand times over that the master was still alive. Their last conversation had been a disaster, Ezra thought. He'd been a spoilt, sulking, stupid child. Ezra felt a prickling behind his eyes and breathed deeply. He was a scientist. Scientists didn't make wishes. Scientists were rational. He sniffed. Since he could no longer speak to the master, he must live to make him proud. Become the best surgeon he could be.

Before the service the crowd had buzzed with so much talk – the loss to the profession, the shock of Mr William McAdam's death, that one of the greats should be felled and killed in his own home by a cracksman… Ezra said nothing. It was no cracksman or common burglar that had killed the master. He sighed, and felt his whole body shudder with grief and with the unfairness of it all.

He forced himself to think of something else; he told himself it was an unfortunate soul who was in need of a surgeon this morning, as the entire Company were here. Dark-coated and hatted, feet yellow with London clay like so many blackbirds, they ranged around the grave of Mr William McAdam, Master Surgeon. There was Mr Gordon from the Middlesex, Mr Ramsay and Mr Hardy from St Thomas's, Mr Franklin from Guy's, as well as Mr Lashley and a good few others Ezra didn't recognize. In the throng of students were a couple of young men who stood out in their manner and dress. These two were dressed in the French style with shortish hair, no wigs, and sombre jackets.

Another stranger stood at the priest's right hand: the master's nephew, Dr James McAdam. Ezra had only met him once, a few years back, and would have been perfectly happy if their paths had never crossed again. He was a physician in Edinburgh whose one answer to all ailments was leeches and yet more leeches. In Ezra's view an excessive reliance on those shiny bloodsuckers had informed the man's character and bearing a good deal.

Dr James had been staying in Great Windmill Street the past two days. In fact, he had settled himself comfortably into the master's rooms on the second floor. His face, unremarkable and white as dirty snow, registered nothing of any interest at all, Ezra thought. He had taken over the running of the household and of the funeral, which Ezra knew for a fact was not what the master had wanted. If Ezra had believed in such things, he would have said the master was spinning in his grave this instant.

As the coffin was lowered, the Company stood in line to walk past and show their respect. Ezra picked up a handful of mud to throw onto the grave, along with a handful of hellebores. The pain in his back flared up as he swung his arm, and he winced and cursed under his breath.

Mrs Boscaven must have heard. She took Ezra's arm and spoke softly. "Now then, Ezra, lad. Don't let the circumstances get the better of you."

"He didn't want this," Ezra said, trying and failing to keep his voice in check. "He told me many times, Mrs B. He wanted to give his body to the science. To be anatomized. To show others there was no harm in it." Ezra knew his voice was getting louder.

Dr James McAdam caught his eye and shook his head at him as if Ezra were nothing more than a naughty child. The anger raged in him and he backed away through the crowd of mourners, out of the graveyard towards town. He would not cry.

He would not cry.

He ran back through the damp grey streets all the way to Great Windmill Street. No one noticed or passed comment. There were close to a million souls in the city, all with their own grievances, their own upsets. So many died every day, he told himself – babies, children – he knew that. He saw his own face reflected in the glass of a shop window on Long Acre. It stopped him short.

There was the scar that defined him, there were his own features, his eyes redder than usual, but there was something else: there was that same madness he'd seen in Miss Loveday Finch's face when he saw her that first time outside Bart's. He rubbed at his eyes, hoping to even out his colour, and hurried home.

"Good service?" Toms asked. He was in the kitchen drinking tea when Ezra came in.

"Not particularly," Ezra said shortly. "Not what the master wanted."

"Way I see it," Toms said, pouring himself another cup, "Master's not here to give a tub of lard what happens to hisself or his house."

"You put it so delicately, Toms."

"I call a spade," he said, looking at Ezra, "a spade." He smiled. "Things will change round here, you see if I'm not wrong."

"Things always change, Toms," Ezra snapped. "That is the nature of life."

"Not our nature, though, yours and mine. We've had the feather-bed life here – you, especially."

Ezra looked away. But Toms went on, "You could have been dead by now if it wasn't for the master. Dead from slave work cutting sugar, dead from dragging a tumour as big as your head around all the day." He paused, then added spitefully, "Although you might have made a deal of coin in a freak show!"

Ezra should have been angry – he *was* angry – but not at Toms. If Toms thought he could get a rise out of him with the same old cheap jabs when the master lay buried in the ground.

"Rest your chops for once, Toms," was all he said, wearily.

Not waiting to hear more from him, Ezra went upstairs, past the mirrors in the hall turned to the wall, through the museum, still shuttered, past the splintered wood and the wall weeping plaster dust where the bullets had done their damage, and into his room.

Toms was right. Everything *would* change. Who knew Dr James's plans? He might sell everything – the museum, the house. Then Ezra would have no job, no home. He knew his heart was hammering just as loudly as it had been the evening those men attacked.

He didn't have many belongings. A few clothes. The most important things were his set of knives and his study books. Ezra began to collect up his notebooks, every one, just in case Dr McAdam packed them away when he wasn't looking. There were years of description of every sort of human body. Those riddled with pox, with palsy; those whose limbs had been eaten away by gangrene. He had seen them all. He tied the notebooks together, tucked them underneath his bed and sat down heavily. Just a few days ago he had thought the navy would be his future. He had never for one second imagined a future without the master.

Before the master's death he had been a child, chasing his own wants and desires. He could see that now. Choice and necessity were opposites indeed. How easy life had seemed such a short time ago.

And money! What would he do to earn a living? He couldn't go right into practice – he had no money for premises or equipment, even if he had more skill than most.

He heard Ellen and Mrs Boscaven arrive back, and Mrs B came up with a cup of tea. She sat down opposite, on his chair, and sighed.

"You away off too?"

"I had thought of it," Ezra said, wiping his face with his sleeve.

"There's no need, lad. Not yet. Nothing's settled."

"Dr James wishes the house sold, does he not? It is as Toms said – we are all of us finished here. Whatever the master may have willed." Ezra tried to keep his voice steady.

"Best not to think too much of the future. Who can say what it might bring?" The ticking of the clock in the museum sounded loud even against the traffic in the street.

"Ez, look, you drink your tea. You have an appointment. You need to get yourself out and off to the master's luncheon."

"At the Company of Surgeons?" Ezra shook his head. "I will not be missed."

"Come now, I can hear the self-pity in your voice. That's not like you, not at all." Mrs Boscaven stood up. "What would the master make of you shut up in your room at a time like this? You owe it to him to go, whatever you might feel for yourself."

"I don't know..."

"Oh, I am right. And look at it this way, with luck and good grace you may even find a new master. If you want to pity anyone, pity Ellen and me, who'll have to rely on Dr James for references." Mrs Boscaven made a face. "The thought of that could make me weep until Wednesday! Get out and put your face about with those surgeons. Speak well of your master to whosoever asks. That's only right. Folk like us cannot afford to weep and wail and gnash our teeth. He was a good man, your master – hold that thought." She patted Ezra on the shoulder. "We must all put on our brave faces, and you must get to the Company before that luncheon is done."

As he left the house, Ezra noticed the strange boy – the dark-haired, dark-eyed boy – hiding in the basement area of Mrs Perino's house. At least, it looked like him from the flash of a glimpse he'd had before the boy ducked down below the level of the street. "Hoi! You! Show yourself! What do you know about the master's death?" Ezra shouted. But no answer came. Ezra opened the area gate and looked down, but the boy seemed to have vanished.

Ezra had never been inside the Company of Surgeons' hall before. He was an apprentice, and on previous visits, delivering messages and suchlike, had had to wait for the master outside. The Company was relatively new, not quite fifty years old, nothing like the medieval wool staplers' or drapers' guilds. The master himself had trained under one of the founder members – a man who had helped set up the Company as separate from barbers and teeth pullers.

"Ours is a new trade," the master liked to say, "at the edge of science!"

Ezra took a deep breath and stepped inside.

Evidently the luncheon had not even begun: he could see the tables set out in the large hall. The party was standing in the lobby drinking wine and talking. Mr Lashley and Dr McAdam appeared very friendly in one corner, the surgeons from Guy's and St Thomas's arguing over knives in another. The two young men in plain jackets and odd haircuts stood on their own.

Ezra walked up to them, his hand out to shake theirs; he hoped his face looked braver than he felt.

"I am Mr Ezra McAdam. I was Mr McAdam's apprentice."

"Ah yes, we have seen you." The shorter man spoke, the accent was French. That would account for their revolutionary hairstyles.

"We were students of Monsieur Desault. I was in London a year ago, for some of his lectures."

"Of course! Last winter. Monsieur Desault." Ezra remembered the name. "The expert on nervous systems. Consciousness and such. The master is – I should say, was – such an admirer of his work! You are both surgeons now?"

The two men nodded.

They seemed quite young, Ezra thought, only a few years older than himself. Perhaps there was hope for him, too.

"Sadly, Monsieur Desault is not well enough to travel." The shorter man paused. "There is a lot of upheaval in France. The revolution, it makes things change quickly, suddenly." He waved his hands. "It can be dangerous, but it is also exciting, yes. Monsieur Desault would have given, how do you say, his whole arm, to pay his respects, to be here."

"You are lucky, I think," the taller man agreed, "to work for Mr McAdam."

"Yes." Ezra swallowed. "Yes, I was."

"Allow me to introduce my colleague, Monsieur Figaud. I am Monsieur Bichat. If ever you are in Paris, we both practise at the Hôtel-Dieu – we would be delighted if you would visit with us, exchange ideas. Surgery is moving so fast in Paris, as is our work on nervous systems – indeed, on the very nature of existence, of life!"

The other man nodded. "We have been experimenting with extending life and consciousness, awareness, with transfusions of blood. We are lucky – or unlucky – to have many, many subjects on which to carry out our experiments."

"Transfusions?" Ezra looked from one man to the other, interested. "I do not think I have ever seen that before."

"You must visit, Mr McAdam," said Monsieur Bichat warmly. "You would be most welcome."

"Thank you, sirs," Ezra said, smiling despite himself. "It sounds most fascinating. Now you must tell me more about your experiments."

The French surgeons were pleased to oblige, and Ezra found their excitement infectious – Monsieur Figaud's eyes lit up as he spoke and Monsieur Bichat displayed an excess of enthusiastic hand gestures. Ezra could not blame them. The thrill of discovery was one he understood only too well. But he kept thinking of the master, how pleased he would have been to hear about this progress … and how much more eagerly he himself would have anticipated a trip to Paris if the master had been coming too.

A waiter brought glasses of wine out on a tray. Ezra took one; he didn't normally drink, but the wine burned his throat and warmed his insides.

"It was a good funeral," Monsieur Bichat said. "I only wish there could have been no funeral at all."

Ezra nodded, staring into his glass.

"But the work must go on," said Monsieur Figaud. "Mr McAdam was a genius. I wish I could have spoken with him about blood supply. We are doing some interesting experiments concerning the exact moment of death and how long the brain remains active."

"Perhaps we could meet again before we leave London?" Monsieur Figaud asked. "We could discuss developments, and visit Mr McAdam's museum, yes?"

"I am not sure if that will be possible," Ezra said. "There was some damage. Some specimens were lost." And, he thought bitterly, I cannot believe Dr James will permit callers.

"*Quel dommage!*" The taller man looked crestfallen.

"Mr McAdam's museum is very famous in France," Monsieur Bichat declared. "Very famous."

Ezra looked over to where Mr Lashley and Dr James were still deep in conversation, heads so close together that he could not help thinking of the double-headed foetus.

"We will not be staying for the luncheon." Monsieur Bichat took out his card. "We have business in town, and then we are leaving for Paris at the end of the week."

Ezra promised to contact them at their hotel if he could arrange a tour of the museum, and he shook their hands as they took their leave. He felt suddenly more terribly alone than ever.

He looked around the room. Mrs Boscaven was usually right. If there was a marketplace for those with his skills he was right at the centre of it now. His eyes lit upon Mr Gordon from the Middlesex Hospital. They had just installed a brand-new theatre for surgery there, and Mr Gordon's reputation was close to the master's. He might make a decent employer. Ezra drank another glass of wine quickly, in two gulps, and started across the room.

"Ah, Ezra McAdam." Ezra turned round. "Just the young man." Dr James was smiling at him. It was not a pleasant sight. Mr Lashley was at his side. On the far side of the room Ezra could see Mr Gordon striking up a conversation with some students. The moment had been lost.

"Dr McAdam, Mr Lashley," Ezra said politely.

"We were just commenting on the funeral service, weren't we, Mr Lashley?"

"Indeed we were, Dr McAdam."

"A fine send-off," Dr James said.

"For a fine surgeon," Lashley added.

Ezra bit his tongue. The way Lashley said it, it sounded like an insult.

"And the memorial will be astounding: Scots granite," Dr James went on. "The Company of Surgeons has got up a subscription."

"I am so glad Dr McAdam is here to see his uncle's estate in order," said Lashley, and Ezra thought the two men ought to compete for the title of oiliest human being in the city of London. "He's been most generous with the contents of the museum. We look forward to finding a home for some of it at St Bartholomew's."

Ezra felt a jolt of shock so real he was sure he must have blanched. "Some of it? Excuse me? I thought the master's will…"

"Don't you worry your woolly head about wills, lad." Dr James turned to Lashley. "I am needed back in Edinburgh – my practice there is among the very best, and it cannot run without me. My uncle would understand."

"Understand what, sir?" Ezra's head was thumping. Perhaps he had drunk the wine too hastily. "His life's work ruined? His wishes for his own death ignored?"

"Do not be impudent with me," Dr James snapped. "Lashley, why you choose to take this boy is beyond me. He can be left out of the settlement if you wish it. You may just take the instruments and the knives—"

"*Take?* I am not a thing!" Ezra exploded. "What settlement is this? Tell me, now!"

"Such a hot head." Lashley tut-tutted. "But he has much skill, Dr McAdam. Your uncle trained him well. He will be a welcome addition to St Bartholomew's."

"What have you done?" Ezra felt his hands balling into fists. He did not know who he wanted to hit first, Dr James or Lashley.

"I do not think this is the time or the place," Dr James hissed. Lashley was smiling. A footman announced that luncheon was served.

Dr James took Ezra's arm and held it tight. "I will see you back at Great Windmill Street," he said, close to his ear. "You may have milked my uncle for all he was worth, inveigled your way into his household and bled him dry all these years, but I assure you I am of a different stamp. He may have been so soft-headed as to have given you his name, but I will have it back." With that he shook Ezra off, turned round and walked away into the dining room.

Ezra was gasping, as stunned as if the blow had been physical. "You can't do this!" He was shouting now, shouting and making a scene in front of every surgeon in the city. "You cannot do this!"

Lashley paused, leant in to Ezra and said quietly but firmly, "You would do well to remember that without your master, a boy like you is so much less than nothing."

Ezra watched as the black-clad crowd went in to eat. There was no way he could put on a brave face and make any kind of small talk now. He felt so sick he thought that if he had been anatomized at that moment his stomach and heart would have shrivelled down even smaller than crab-apples. His brain was buzzing in his head. The ground seemed to have shifted under his feet; the whole world had been tilted into wrongness.

How could it happen that men like that walked and his master lay dead?

Chapter Nine

Mr William McAdam's Anatomy School and
Museum of Curiosities
Great Windmill Street
Soho
London
November 1792

By the time he had reached Great Windmill Street Ezra felt numb, and not just with cold.

But there was Miss Loveday Finch, standing on the step, tomato-soup-red curls escaping from her black bonnet. She turned and began speaking as soon as she saw him. "I have been waiting close to half an hour and no one is in. I was almost worried! I have made you an appointment with Mr Falcon. We should go there now."

Her chatter seemed to come to him as if muffled through a heavy cloth. Ezra shook his head. "I am in no fit state, Miss Finch." He took out his key and unlocked the door. "Although you are obviously in the pink of health," he observed. "I see you are not using your stick."

She stopped for a moment, her expression softening slightly. "I know your master died," she said. She seemed awkward; perhaps she did not know what to say when someone else was in mourning. "It has been all over the newspapers. I suppose," she went on, apparently unable to keep herself from talking regardless, "if you are shot with a gun then it's so obviously murder that the world sits up and takes notice, as opposed to merely being poisoned. They have arrested one of the culprits, the gunman – a man by the name of Ahmat – have you heard? I expect they will call you as a witness."

"Ahmat," Ezra repeated, interested in spite of himself. "That was his name. Is there a trial set?"

She flapped a hand. "He is sure to hang! They say he is Turkish, formerly with the Ottoman ligation." She leant close, lowered her voice. "Don't you see how it all knits together? We have to go to the embassy, as you said. Something is rotten there, something that caused my father's death and that of the tongueless man, which led to the murder of your master!"

"It is possible," Ezra said slowly, stepping inside. "But at present nothing much seems to matter."

Miss Finch put a gloved hand on his shoulder. "Listen to me, Ezra McAdam, I do understand how you must feel. And if there is one thing I have learnt from my own recent bereavement, it is that one should do everything one can to make oneself busy."

"It is not at all that simple," said Ezra wearily, pushing her hand away.

She was undeterred. "Mr McAdam, there is always something one can do."

She followed him inside and down to the kitchen, and against his better judgement he told her everything. Miss Finch was suitably shocked. She made tea while he spoke.

"The master's nephew is even selling his instruments – his knives," Ezra finished with a sigh. "I know this sounds selfish, but I swear they were promised to me." He shook his head. "As it is, he even wants his precious name back! Well, he can have it. I cannot think of anything worse than sharing a name with that snake. He has me in a corner and I can see no way out – if I wish to continue as a surgeon I must see out my apprenticeship with Mr Lashley."

"Is he quite as bad as you paint him?" she asked.

Ezra gave her a look.

Miss Finch was unusually quiet for some time. Then she finished her tea and looked directly at Ezra.

"I understand how things must seem to you now, but –" Ezra went to interrupt but Miss Finch put her hand up – "people are strange things and often say one thing then do another. I was, if you will remember, the Spirit of Truth." Ezra sighed but let her continue. "What you must remember is that however kindly Mr McAdam treated you when he was alive, he may not have thought as far ahead as his own death."

"But he did!" Ezra said hotly. "Have you not been listening at all? His legacy, his research – he made provision. I know it. He had lawyers, in Middle Temple Inn, and Dr James has never mentioned them once."

"There is little point in directing your fury at me, Ezra McAdam." Ezra could see she was determined. "You are in a fix and, worse, you are laid low by grief. The only way out is for us to *do* something about it."

Ezra spluttered, his tea shooting out of his mouth. "Us?" he said. "In what capacity is there an *us*?"

"Finch and McAdam," she said firmly, getting up. "As I said before. And it seems we have a deal of work: my father's killers, the tongueless man – who, I think we both agree, is the linchpin to these strange events – the little boy who came looking for him… You know, I think I may have seen him on the green outside Mrs Gurney's."

"You too?" Ezra was surprised. "I thought I saw him across the street this morning. I imagined I was seeing things."

"And now we have to deal with your master's final will and testament, too."

Ezra frowned. "Do you honestly think…?"

Miss Finch looked at him. "Yes, I do. Now, you will have to buck up, Mr McAdam – or whatever you choose to call yourself in future. You were right, you do need to quiz Mr Falcon. I saw him at Pa's funeral and he looked very strange, not like himself at all." She clapped her hands. "Come along, then, there is much work to be done."

Ezra followed her back out into the afternoon damp. Miss Finch spoke all the time of her theories on death and bereavement, which she had decided she would write down as a book and perhaps make her fortune. By the time they had reached the magician's house on St Martin's Lane, Ezra found himself smiling.

Miss Finch knocked at the door of a thin, slightly run-down townhouse. "Are you laughing at me, Ezra McAdam?" she demanded. "If you are…"

"No, absolutely not!" he said. "Not laughing, merely smiling. And you should be pleased – you have almost banished my gloomy spirits."

The door opened. "We are here to see Mr Falcon," Miss Finch said.

The landlady stood aside and let them in. "He's on the second floor. But I've not seen hide nor hair of him since last night. I think he might have been entertaining, if you get my drift."

"What does she mean?" Ezra asked as they climbed the stairs.

"Mr Falcon is fond of the ladies," Miss Finch whispered back.

The house was clean but shabby, and Ezra wondered why Mr Falcon, without the financial burden of a daughter, should live in lodgings so much poorer than those of Mr Finch.

"Here." Loveday Finch knocked at the door. There was no answer. She knocked again and called out, "It's Loveday, Mr Falcon, sir!"

Still nothing. She turned to Ezra. "He promised me he would see us at two o'clock." Her face looked suddenly pale, bloodless.

Ezra knocked this time, and much harder, but there was still no reply. "Perhaps he has gone out," he said. "Perhaps he had other business to attend to?"

Miss Finch shook her head. "The landlady said he has not been seen at all. I will go and speak to her. Perhaps she will let me have a key." She disappeared down the stairs before Ezra could protest, leaving him alone at the door. Ezra hoped the man had *not* been entertaining; he could not think what he would do if they opened the door and Mr Falcon was not alone. He knocked again, for good measure – still nothing.

Miss Finch returned triumphant a few minutes later, the key gleaming in her hand. "I gave her a shilling for it."

The room was dark, the curtains not drawn; there was a smell, the rancid, sharp smell of stale vomit. The bed, at first, seemed an untidy pile of coats and clothes. Loveday Finch gasped.

"Oh Lord! He's here!"

Ezra pulled the curtains, and there on the bed, mouth open as if drowning in air, lay the blanched corpse of Mr Edward Falcon.

Chapter Ten

Mrs Carradine's Theatrical Boarding House
St Martin's Lane
London
November 1792

"You sure he's dead? He was as well as a body can be only yesterday!" The landlady stood at the side of Mr Falcon's bed, hands on her hips. "Who's to deal with the man now? Are you family? If you are, you had best get him out before nightfall, I don't fancy as having a dead man as a lodger. As far as I know, dead men are particularly bad at paying rent."

"I..." Ezra glanced at Loveday, but her eyes were fixed on the bed, on what had been Mr Falcon, and she did not hear him. "Madam," he asked, composing himself a little, "did you see any other person enter or leave Mr Falcon's rooms? You said he might have had company?"

The landlady made a face. "I never actually saw the girl – if it *was* a girl, you understand. I just heard footsteps, heard all sorts of bangings, I did, but I keeps my mouth shut and my eyes closed I do."

"Is that really all you have to say about it?" Loveday burst out, finally tearing her gaze away from the body, her face flushed with indignation. "This was *murder*!"

"Whatever it was, I want nothing to do with it," the landlady sniffed.

Loveday opened her mouth again but Ezra held out a hand and shook his head. She subsided, looking miserable.

Ezra ushered the landlady away with promises that they would deal with Mr Falcon's rent and his belongings, and gave her instructions to send a boy to fetch the local coroner at Covent Garden. Loveday sat down in the one chair, set in front of a mean little writing desk. She looked numb with shock. Ezra thought it best to let her be, and checked the corpse's pulse just in case. He stood back, then regarded in close detail what had once been a man.

The body lay fully clothed on top of the bed, still in mourning from Mr Finch's funeral by the looks of things. A hat was thrown down upon the floor; a bottle of second-rate gin and a plate of half-eaten pastries stood on the bedside table.

"Honey cakes." Ezra picked them up and smelt them.

Loveday Finch sniffed and wiped her tears away. She looked at them and then at Ezra. "Baklava."

Ezra nodded, wrapped them in his handkerchief and tucked them into his jacket pocket. "I'll take them back to the laboratory."

Although he was pretty sure of the cause of Mr Falcon's death, Ezra rolled back the corpse's shirt and looked for wounds or bruising at his wrists, or on his neck or torso. Nothing. Only crumbs across the man's waistcoat and the smell of spirits on his breath. Ezra sniffed the gin, too, but there was nothing out of the ordinary there.

"Poison!" Miss Finch declared. "In those cakes, no doubt, like with Pa. Yesterday he was alive and well – he walked, he talked. He spoke the eulogy at Pa's funeral!"

"Poison, yes. I would put money on it," Ezra said. "Miss Finch, please look round the room. Does anything seem different? Is anything moved, or out of the ordinary? We must look hard."

Miss Finch shook her head. "I cannot say. I never was in his lodgings before, not in London – although," she added, "it always struck me, when we were travelling, that he was most fastidious, most tidy."

"Then someone has already been through his things," Ezra said.

"I think they might have been," Miss Finch agreed thoughtfully, getting up at last.

"Look in his coat pockets and in his drawers – let us see if anything will put us on the path towards whoever may be the cause of this disaster."

Loveday nodded and began to search.

In the chamberpot underneath the bed Ezra found the vomit. The man had been sick, and with no one to care for him or call a doctor, he had died alone. Ezra picked up a pen from the man's writing desk, then bent down and poked at the vomit with it – there were the tell-tale green flecks of pistachio nut. Where in heaven's name had he got the honey cakes? Had someone delivered them? Had he called on the embassy?

Miss Finch had opened the top drawer of the chest of drawers. She pushed aside the socks and underthings and pulled out the paper that had been used to line the drawer. There, at the back, was a small square of writing paper, folded over four times.

She smiled triumphantly. "It was where my pa hid things too," she said, but when they unfolded it they found it was only notes for a new trick: a diagram of a box with a false wall that could be used to make things vanish. There was nothing else in any of the other drawers but in Mr Falcon's jacket pocket she found a small notebook containing addresses of various patrons they had worked for in Vienna and Paris and Constantinople. In a trouser pocket Ezra found a receipt from a chop house in Long Acre, the business card of a Russian fur importer near London Bridge and a folded-up letter addressed to Mr Edward Falcon.

"This is Papa's handwriting!" Loveday opened it quickly and then sat down again, deflated. "It is in Arabic," she said.

"Did your father speak Arabic?" asked Ezra, looking at it over her shoulder. "Or Mr Falcon?"

"A little – please and thank you. Mr Falcon could not manage even that. I never saw my father write it, though." She sighed. "Why on earth should he write to Mr Falcon in a language neither of them could understand?"

"It might tell us something of use," Ezra mused, "if only we could read the thing. Nothing seems clear at all!"

"One thing is clear," Loveday said quietly. "Mr Falcon is gone. He was like an uncle to me, and now he is dead. I have no family, no work now, nothing at all!" She sat in the chair, her hands folded uselessly in her lap, the very picture of misery. Then suddenly her eyes grew wide and she leant forward. "Who's to say that I will not be next?

That someone will not poison *me*?" She gasped. "That they have not already set the hour of my death!"

Ezra grimaced. She was over-dramatic, but she was right. "Miss Finch, I'm sure—"

"How can you be sure of anything any more? Oh, I wish I had my blade!"

Ezra did not think her blade would be much good against poison, but he did not say so. "We need to find out who did this and why," he said firmly. He cast around the room. "There must be *something* here."

"We have looked! We have looked everywhere. We are magicians, Ezra, that's all. Why poison magicians?"

"The coroner's men will be here soon to collect the body. We already have an idea of how the death was caused, just not why. If we can only find the why…"

"We?" she said, a little hope breaking into her voice.

"Yes," Ezra said with a smile. "We, Finch and McAdam – or Finch and whatever my new name will be." He looked at her. She was smiling a little more. Good.

The coroner's men came swiftly and bore the body away to the crypt of St Peter's. Ezra thought he should like to be present at the post-mortem, to take a good look at the man's heart. Miss Finch told the landlady she could have Mr Falcon's good cloak and boots to pay for another week's rent. Then she and Ezra would go through the man's rooms with a fine-toothed comb.

They went and sat together in the tea rooms in Panton Street, Ezra with his notebook, Miss Finch with a battered leather-bound book that had belonged to her father. It was best to do this methodically – and Ezra was aware that his own future was far from clear at present, so they may as well get as much as they could done while they could.

They went over the events of the past few days again and again. The tongueless man, the honey cakes, the master's killer, the Arabic letter.

"There is a definite Ottoman connection but it still doesn't make sense," Ezra said. "I swear the man Oleg is Russian, but a Russian working with the Turks? I thought those two countries were enemies."

"He may have his own reasons for all we know."

Ezra looked at Loveday. She was right. "There must be something we are missing. The master used to say violent death was either within families or to do with money."

"My father and I had no money problems," Loveday said, "and I have always done the accounts. I would have known."

"What about Mr Falcon?"

Loveday shrugged. "They shared all income."

"Equally?" Ezra asked.

"Yes, down the middle. If anything he should have been better off than us."

Ezra asked Miss Finch to find and check Mr Falcon's accounts and to write as thorough and complete a memoir of their time in Constantinople as possible; there may have been someone offended somehow, perhaps. If she wrote the memory down, start to finish, something might turn up.

"And the translation, of course – we need to read that letter," Ezra added. "Perhaps someone at the embassy could translate it for you. Who was it you performed for?"

"A Mr Ali Pasha. Father was on good terms with him.

Perhaps..." She frowned, firm with a sudden resolve. "We should speak with him. As soon as possible – today."

"Miss Finch," Ezra began, but he could see she was already set on it.

Oh well. It could not be so difficult, he thought; and it would do them both good to get some answers for once.

The embassy building was a brand-new white-stuccoed palace in the grandest part of town. As they crossed the street Ezra could feel his resolve fading, but he steeled himself and made for the entrance.

"Ezra, wait!" Loveday grabbed him by the elbow before he could reach the door. "The tradesmen's entrance," she said, "not the main one. If anybody here is to recognize me it is far more likely it will be there."

"*If?*" Ezra hissed. "You never said *if* before, Miss Finch! If this is some wild-goose chase—"

"Then neither of us will have lost anything by it! And in any case someone is bound to know me. I am very memorable."

Ezra couldn't argue with that, at least.

The porter did not know Loveday.

"Of Falcon and Finch," she clarified when he simply shook his head at her. "We performed for Mr Ali Pasha. He was in correspondence with my father, who has been murdered. It is most urgent we speak with him."

"Impossible," said the porter, waving a hand dismissively. "Mr Ali Pasha is an important man, and very busy. Whatever it is you want with him, he has no time—"

"I already told you!" Loveday protested. "It is a serious matter. My father has been murdered – and Mr

Falcon too – and I am sure if your Mr Ali Pasha knew of it he would be keen to help us clear the matter up."

The porter sniffed. "I think not, Miss. He has better things to do than attend to a girl's flights of fancy."

Loveday bristled, and Ezra thought he had better intervene. "Sir, please…" he began, but the porter had already closed the door on them.

Loveday was fuming as they left, but Ezra felt only a resigned disappointment. It was as if every way they looked there were only dead ends and false hopes.

"There must be someone else in the whole of London who speaks Arabic," he said, trying not to sound as weary as he felt. "We will get to the root of it, Miss Finch."

Loveday sighed, some of the fire leaving her. She was tired, too. "Of course. I will make enquiries."

"And are you sure you'll be safe at Mrs Gurney's? It might be an idea to find other lodgings."

"I couldn't stomach more change," Loveday confessed. "I will be careful what I eat, and I will have my blade – I am pretty good with that, you know."

"I don't doubt it."

"And anyway, where would I go?" She shrugged. "I must make the best of things. Keep busy, find the root of all this trouble. I am sure we will, eventually." But she sighed again, heavily, and did not sound convinced.

"We will, I promise."

"Thank you, Ezra. I don't know what I'd do…" Her voice trailed off. "I must put on a smile, that's what I must do. It will all work out, I am sure."

She thanked him again as they reached Clerkenwell Green, said she would think on anything or anyone odd that she and her father had happened upon during their trip to Constantinople. Ezra said he would attend the coroner's post-mortem. He bade her farewell and turned back towards Great Windmill Street.

It was already getting dark and Ezra ran all the way home. He stopped on the front step, took a honey cake out of his pocket and broke it in half. He was putting one half of it in one of Mrs Boscaven's mousetraps in the kitchen when Toms came in swinging a small carpetbag.

Ezra put the trap down close to the hole in the skirting nearest to the fireplace.

"You off somewhere?" he said to Toms.

"I'm not staying here, I know that much. And in your shoes I'd be making plans too."

"Why's that?" Ezra asked. "I know the master's will – he spoke of it. He wished the anatomy school to continue."

"He's dead, Ez," Toms said flatly. Ezra bridled, but Toms didn't notice. "You and I have seen the nephew. Even I can tell he's not one who is," Toms paused, looking for the right word, "a generous man. He'll be rid of all of us before long, mark my words. What the master willed is neither here nor there … not when he's not here to make it so."

Ezra remembered the funeral, and nodded sadly. The thought chilled him. Everything would change completely. He hadn't fully taken it in. The master had been both teacher and parent.

He turned away so Toms wouldn't see his face.

"And there were solicitor's men round the house, making lists while you lot was out." Toms drained his cup. "I'm off looking for work back up in Hampstead.

I liked it there. Clean air. No bodies lying around or jars full of bits."

"The museum is important, the exhibits should stay together." As Ezra said the words he remembered this afternoon. Lashley and Dr James seemed to have made their plans.

"Well, I wouldn't put it past that Scotchman to flog the whole lot off and pocket the rhino himself." Toms put his cup down and held his hand out. "Shake? I know I ribbed you, but it were only talk. You weren't too bad for a darkie," he said. "No hard feelings?"

Ezra shook Toms's hand. He knew he ought to feel pleased to see the back of him, but he didn't. Toms' going was just one more thing changing, another part of his old life about to disappear. Ezra said nothing, just watched as Toms walked away down the street and off into a new life. Whistling, carefree.

It was nearly seven o'clock and Ezra was helping Mrs Boscaven lay the table for the servants' tea when Dr James called down that a messenger had arrived for Ezra. Ezra went up to the master's office, but when Dr James handed it over, he saw that the envelope had already been torn open.

"Sir!" Ezra said. "You have opened my post!"

"This is my house," Dr James snapped. "You have my name. Do not worry, I am not interested in your comings and goings, but you would do well to tell your young lady friend you are not going anywhere now, for if you do, know that the door will be locked for the evening. This is not a hotel or a lodging house."

Dr James slammed the door to the master's office, leaving Ezra standing in the hall holding his letter. He took it out and read it.

Meet me tonight at the corner of Coldbath Fields,
9.00 p.m. URGENT. I talked with the boy. It is
imperative you come. Will explain all later.
Miss L. Finch

Ezra looked from the letter with its scrawled lines to the tight-shut door of the master's old office. The word "urgent" was capitalized in Loveday Finch's sloping hand. He had no choice but to go.

Ezra hardly ate any tea, and left with plenty of time to make it the mile or so to Coldbath Fields, just north of Clerkenwell. He took his pocket knife and notebook, his tinderbox and a half-shilling, in case of some kind of emergency.

As Ezra made his way east through the dark city streets there was the thinnest sliver of moon and only one house in four had bothered to put out a lantern. But the darkness and the candles lit inside meant Ezra could see into houses as he passed by. Not the parlours or the drawing rooms on the upper floors – those had their heavy winter curtains pulled shut to keep out the cold – but the kitchen windows, on which no such curtains were wasted. Little glimpses of lives lived in basements from Holborn all the way almost to Islington, entire households of servants busy with cooking or, having finished work, sitting with their feet up close to the fire, warm and cosy, talking and laughing. Ezra shivered, and it wasn't just the cold: he felt completely and utterly alone.

He passed the brewery at the end of Liquorpond Street and then the roads turned to mud. Up ahead out of the dark loomed Coldbath Fields Prison, square and heavy, rising up out of the fields like a prison ship that had broken upon the land, as if reminding all around that hell existed here on earth.

Ezra looked up at the bowl of dark blue sky and wondered what path had led him into this terrible tangle of poison and murder. He hoped his master was somewhere safe and peaceful now.

"There you are!" Loveday Finch appeared suddenly out of the shadows. She was holding a spade and had some kind of heavy bag across her shoulder. There was a boy with her, short, no more than nine or ten, carrying nothing. It was, Ezra realized as he came closer, the boy he'd seen outside the house on two occasions – the boy with the strange enunciation and ragged clothes who'd asked about the tongueless cadaver.

Loveday must have seen the look on Ezra's face. "This is Mahmoud," she said. Mahmoud nodded slightly. She went on, "I found him lurking outside Mrs Gurney's. He has been following us."

Ezra stared at Mahmoud, who looked unrepentant. "I knew it!"

"He is a prince," Loveday said matter-of-factly. "Come along, I have a spade." She and the boy moved further off into the dark.

"A prince?" Ezra hurried to keep up with her. "A spade? What on earth is happening? Where are we going?"

"My father's grave!" Loveday called over her shoulder.

"We have to open the coffin. We need to look at the body."

"Wait! Miss Finch, may I remind you that I was present at his –" he paused; he didn't like to say it – "his, um, examination by Mr Lashley."

"We have to dig him up. You need to look again, Mahmoud says it is important."

"Imperative," Mahmoud added.

"'Mahmoud says' what? *Mahmoud*," Ezra hissed, "is a boy."

"A boy," Loveday replied, wheeling round, "who is the fifth son of the Ottoman Emperor Selim the Third! This is about money, as you predicted, and the money is on my father's body. Mahmoud says he will translate my letter as soon as we dig up my father for him."

Ezra put his hand on her shoulder. "I told you, there was nothing on his body, or inside it!"

The boy piped up, his voice strange and clear despite his foreign accent and much too grand for a ten-year-old dressed in ragged clothes and smelling as if he'd not washed in some time.

"They are mine," he declared. "The Cherries of Edirne. My insurance, which I need sorely, circumstances being what they are, and her father was to bring them to me."

"Cherries?" Ezra frowned.

"Rubies!" Miss Finch said.

"The man who killed the master wanted rubies, I remember!" Ezra's mind was racing. "But how…?"

Loveday shook him off. "It will take too long to explain now, and there is no time – someone else may get there first. There are jewels, Mr McAdam, hidden about my father's body. We have to get them before anyone else and we have to do this now. That is at the heart of the whole mystery!"

"I told you," Ezra said firmly, "I was there when Mr Finch was opened up. There was nothing there – his stomach was already gone—"

"They were hidden under his skin," interrupted the boy, "not in his stomach."

"Well, that's all right then!" Ezra snapped. "Of course! Oh, I remember, we failed to take his brain or bowels apart. Perhaps they were stuck up his—"

"Mr McAdam! Please!" Loveday had thrown down the spade and was using her hands to cover the boy's ears.

Ezra recovered himself. "I am sorry. I was just saying that we – I – would have found anything."

"I think not," Mahmoud said. He seemed remarkably composed. "We have ways and means. The jewels were to be hidden under the skin of his scalp, just behind the ear."

"See?" Miss Finch took Ezra's hand impatiently. "Come along!"

Chapter Eleven

St James's Churchyard
New Prison Walk
Clerkenwell
London
November 1792

A graveyard at night is always eerie, Ezra thought, even when a corpse is a normal part of your work. There was no one in the watch house, but given the cold night it was not surprising.

Miss Finch handed Ezra the spade. "You are the biggest, and Mahmoud is a prince."

"That is no excuse for not digging!"

Mahmoud looked at him, and even in the dark Ezra was certain the boy's lip curled. "Are you a republican, then?"

"Isn't this whole debacle due to the whims of sultans and princes? Surely if your countrymen governed themselves…"

Mahmoud drew himself up to his full height. "You know nothing of my countrymen!"

"No politics," Loveday hissed. "Not now."

Ezra shook his head. What in heaven's name was he

doing hanging around in a dark, cold graveyard arguing with a boy who said he was a prince?

"This is madness, Miss Finch," he said.

Loveday led him aside. "Please, I know it sounds outlandish, even to me, but I do believe him. Do you think I would countenance digging up the body of my own father if I did not?"

Ezra could not argue with that. "Keep a good watch, then – if anyone sees, we are in trouble."

"I thought you said taking a corpse was not a crime," Loveday said.

"Yes, but opening up a grave is." Ezra started digging anyway. "One other thing, Miss Finch," he said, "this will not be an easy thing... Your father has been dead for some time, and—"

"I am a grown woman, Mr McAdam. I know what we are about. Do not baby me."

The digging was not hard, as the grave had only been filled the previous day. Ezra struck the coffin before long, and called for the boy – prince or not – to jump down with him and help clear the dirt off the top.

The coffin was sealed. Ezra took out his pocket knife, which was sharp enough to break the seal but not thick enough to lever the coffin open. Instead he used the edge of the spade, once, twice. The third time he heard the wood splinter.

The smell was the usual reek of damp earth and rotting meat. Mahmoud jumped up as there wasn't room in the grave for both of them and the coffin lid. Miss Finch stepped away.

"Is he there? Is it him?" she whispered.

"We need the lamp," Ezra called up.

Loveday passed it down, and Ezra set it on a ledge of clay and began to undo the winding sheet from the top, just as far as the neck.

Mr Finch, thanks to the cold weather, didn't look too bad save for the flesh beginning to draw back from the mouth and the eyes beginning to sink – where the balls had softened slightly, Ezra reckoned.

"So where am I looking?" he asked.

"Behind the right ear," the boy answered.

Ezra turned the head – he felt the give of the flesh in the neck, and pulled it away. Under his fingers the skin felt clay-cold, putty-soft. He moved the ear, hoping it wouldn't come away in his hand – the skin had begun to slip from the cadaver. He felt behind it.

"Have you found anything?" Loveday called.

"There!" A lump, two, underneath his fingertips. He took his pocket knife and sliced the skin. There was no blood. Three flat, slippery, disc-shaped stones slid into his open hand. "I have them!"

Suddenly there was the sound of slow hooves on the ground and the wheels of a large heavy cart somewhere out on the road. Loveday squealed and threw herself and the boy into the grave with Ezra.

"Are you *mad*?" Ezra hissed.

"Someone is coming, I know it!"

Ezra snuffed out the lamp and the three of them froze, as still as Mr Finch, lying beside them in the dark.

The cart seemed to move agonizingly slowly. Ezra was intensely conscious of the face of the cadaver only inches from his own, and his own breathing sounded so loud he was certain it must somehow be heard from the road. He held his breath, his heart pounding in his chest, and after an age the hoofbeats receded into the night.

"I smell of death," Loveday said as she scrambled out, shaking her skirts to loosen the mud. Ezra shut the coffin lid as best he could and clambered out after her, slipping and sliding on the mud.

"You found them?" the boy demanded.

"I found something. Look." Ezra unclenched his fist and the stones, no bigger than marbles, glistened in his palm, even in the dim moonlight.

"Oi! Who's there?" A call from beyond the churchyard wall – a man, the watch, with a lantern raised.

Ezra felt his heart skip. He looked at Loveday Finch and Mahmoud. But in an instant the boy had snatched up the stones from his hand and run – vanished, as quick as a phantom, into the dark.

Miss Finch grabbed Ezra's hand and pulled him into the shadow of the church.

"Is someone there? Oi!" the watch called again. He blew his whistle in alarm – there was the distant sound of boots on cobbles; the man wasn't alone.

"We've had it!" Ezra whispered.

"Come on! Over the wall and into the fields!" Loveday Finch began to run.

"What about the boy?"

"This way!" They got as far as the wall but it seemed to be higher here. Ezra thought he might be able to scramble up, but Miss Finch in her skirts would be trapped.

Behind them they could hear footsteps and a dog barking, coming closer all the while.

Loveday turned to him and grinned. "Come here!" she said, and pulled Ezra into a clinch.

"What?" The word came out distinctly muffled as she launched herself at him, and Ezra found Loveday Finch's lips pressed to his. It was, he thought, infinitely more shocking than disinterring a corpse ever could be.

The watchman swung his lantern towards them and stopped. The light was strong and yellow and they broke apart, blinking.

"It's only a pair of young 'uns!" the watchman called over his shoulder. "You seen anything? Grave over there's been disturbed." The man swung his lantern around, and Ezra was glad that Loveday had left the spade.

"No, sir. Sorry, sir," Ezra said, hoping the mud that clung to their shoes would not give them away.

"Get on with you," the man said. "Go on. Quick, before I change my mind and lock you up for something I haven't thought of yet."

"Yes, sir. Thank you, sir." Ezra took Loveday's hand in his and they ran towards the gate and out into the fields, keeping the pace up until they saw the lights of the houses at Clerkenwell Green in the distance.

"I am never doing that again!" Ezra panted, stamping his feet as soon as they reached the modern stone paving to dislodge the grave mud from his boots. Every bone ached from digging, his fingers were greasy with corpse residue and his lips felt as if they had been assaulted.

"The watch let us alone, didn't they?" Loveday said, almost giggling with relief.

"Thank heavens! But where did the boy go?"

"Mahmoud? I think he got away. I hope so. Perhaps

he will come to the house tomorrow."

"Why?" Ezra asked. "He has what he wants – you and I taken for mugs and doing his dirty work. That is royalty through and through."

"But don't you see?" said Loveday. "This is the answer to everything! Someone knew Pa was carrying those rubies but whoever killed him couldn't find them." She looked at Ezra. "Those things must have been worth a fortune – that's why they took his body! And when they still found nothing they went after Mr Falcon…"

"Why would your father do that? Carry those things under his skin?" Ezra made a face.

"We do not all have a trade, Ezra McAdam. Money comes and goes. Pa would have accepted the fee." Loveday paused. "What I still don't see, though, is why they came after your master."

Ezra frowned. "It was the tongueless man they sought. When I first met Mahmoud he thought the Negro might have had a letter on him – perhaps it would have been important?"

"I don't think Mahmoud should be in this country at all." Loveday was getting carried away, leaping from one thought to the next without provocation; it was as if Ezra hadn't said anything at all. "That's what he told me. His grandmother, the valide sultan, sent him here in secret, to go to school, to escape the fate of all those princes locked away in the harem. To escape madness."

Ezra shook his head. "Perhaps those princes do not have it all their own way," he acknowledged.

"They are only let out into the world once they become sultan. It's to prevent intrigue. One party favouring one prince would poison all the others..." She trailed off. "Someone in the embassy," she went on, "Ahmat, perhaps, must have found out that Mahmoud was here and not safely locked up in Constantinople."

"But why would the Ottomans want to kill one of their own?" Ezra asked.

"This is intrigue of the highest order, don't you see? The Russian Empire has been chipping away at its Ottoman neighbours for years. Turkey grows weak. The Russians, Pa told me, want the Black Sea, want the Bosphorus. They would do anything to have their man, a puppet sultan, on the Ottoman throne. Definitely not Mahmoud, a boy who has seen the world, grown up outside the Cage; who refused to be told what to do by another country."

Ezra smiled to himself at the idea of the imperious Mahmoud being told what to do by anyone. Then another thought occurred to him. "So that's why Oleg is working with Mr Ahmat – a Russian and a Turk!"

"Yes! If they kill Mahmoud here in London, no one will be any the wiser – after all, he should be at home in the Topkapi Palace surrounded by servants and flunkies. And Ahmat would have the rubies."

"So he hides on the streets..."

They reached the doorstep of Mrs Gurney's house. Ezra could see a light burning in the horrible yellow drawing room.

"I would invite you in," Loveday said, "but Mrs Gurney rather took against you. If I hear from Mahmoud I will send word. I have no doubt he will be in touch." Ezra made a face. Loveday shrugged. "He is a prince."

"He is in hiding!" Ezra hissed.

"He needs us. What can a street boy do with a handful of rubies?" She shivered. "I must go in and change. We can talk tomorrow if you like."

Ezra was exhausted, and the thought of going back to Great Windmill Street and all the uncertainty that awaited him there made him feel heavy.

"I cannot say, Miss Finch. I do not know where or what I will be doing tomorrow," he began, but Loveday had already turned the lock in the door and pushed it open.

"Good night," she said, and was gone.

Ezra realized quite suddenly how cold he felt. The master dead. Anna gone. Was there any point to anything? He stood still on Miss Finch's doorstep, listening to her call to Mrs Gurney that she was home then pull the bolt on the other side of the door. The church at St James's on the green struck eleven. If he hurried, perhaps Mrs Boscaven or Ellen would still be up and able to let him in by the area door.

The next morning, the jaunt in the graveyard seemed like part of a very strange dream, but there was still the remnant of the yellow London clay on Ezra's shoes to prove otherwise. For a few seconds he had seen those rubies; felt them in his hand. He smiled. Anna would never believe the tale in a thousand years.

When he sat up he realized Ellen hadn't laid or lit the fire, which was strange, and when he opened the curtain he could tell by the height of the sun behind the cloud that it must be late. He listened for other sounds in the house but could hear nothing. He washed and dressed quickly, and went downstairs.

In the kitchen there was no sign of anybody at all – the stillness was almost unsettling. It wasn't until Ezra went into the hall that he found Dr James with Ellen and Mrs Boscaven and their bags, packed, ready to leave. Ellen was teary and clung to Mrs B, who patted her shoulder consolingly and looked at Ezra with regret.

Dr James took out his pocket watch, eyebrows arched. "What time do you call this?"

Ezra opened his mouth – what on earth was happening? – but Dr James shushed him. "I leave for Edinburgh in a while, and the house is to be shut up. Fetch your bag and come with me."

"What?" Ezra said. "Am I to go to Scotland?"

"Don't be an idiot, boy. I do not want you. You have a place with Mr Lashley. Though I doubt with all my heart that you deserve it."

Ezra knew his heart was still beating, but he felt frozen. Already?

"Well, get about your business! I haven't got all day, and if you think I am leaving you in the house to close up and to take still more liberties with the McAdam family, you are utterly and completely mistaken."

Chapter Twelve

Surgeon's Operating Theatre
St Bartholomew's Hospital
Smithfield
London
November 1792

The subject was a girl, not twenty, her face white as clean linen and her knee a mangled mess of bone and sinew. Ezra had asked the porter about her; he said she was a girl who cried apples and pears in the street who'd got caught under the wheels of a runaway timber wagon coming down Fish Street Hill.

From the hallway outside the operating theatre Ezra could hear the cry of a baby. The porter said it had been strapped to the young woman's back when it happened, and was lucky not to have been injured.

Ezra had tied the tourniquet tightly around the girl's thigh, and there was not so much bleeding. She had been strapped down to the table, and – poor thing, Ezra thought – was still completely conscious, even though she stank to high heaven of gin. She was mumbling prayers under her breath, and when Ezra came close she grabbed his wrist.

"I have never seen so many gentlemen all in one place," she whispered. "Perhaps there is one who'll want to wed a one-legged maid?" Ezra looked at her properly. She was passing fair: dark hair, brown eyes – like Anna, he thought.

"Perhaps," he said, and looked away.

"Sir, young sir!" she called him back. "Tell me, will I live?" Ezra could hear the desperation and fear cracking her voice.

"Of course," he said with as much warmth as he could muster in the cold room. He gave her a reassuring smile.

He was lying. He could not know for certain; this was his first operation as Mr Lashley's assistant. He had never seen the man's knives go to work on living flesh, but having seen him ruin a cadaver the thought was chilling. Ezra hoped he had hidden those thoughts from her. He offered her some laudanum but she wanted only more gin. He sent a porter out for a quart and hoped it would come quickly. He wished that Josiah, Lashley's old apprentice, was here, but Ezra had heard that he'd run off to join the army before Lashley could get rid of him.

The operating theatre was filled to bursting. The noise of the gentlemen's chatter and the smoke from their pipes rose up and gathered against the ceiling. Ezra laid out the surgeon's instruments: flesh knives, bone saw, artery hook. Of course, they weren't Lashley's – they were the master's, and consequently old friends. He had spent the morning sharpening and cleaning them, and they gleamed. Ezra checked and tightened the girl's straps and laid out the padding and bandages for afterwards.

The doors swung open and Mr Lashley entered, hat

off, grinning. Ezra helped him on with his apron. He wasn't certain, but he thought that Mr Lashley smelt of spirits too. The crowd fell into silence.

"Gentlemen, scholars!" Lashley announced. "I am taking off the limb here, above the knee. I will be quick, and it will be efficiently and neatly done." He waved a hand towards Ezra. "You may have noticed Ezra McWilliam, lately the apprentice of the most esteemed William McAdam."

Ezra looked from Mr Lashley to the crowd in surprise, and blinked. He still was not used to the new name. He had changed it as Dr James had promised legal action should he not, and he thought it still reflected the high respect in which he held his old master.

Whatever his name, he was not used to being made the centre of attention, not at all.

"Gentlemen," Mr Lashley said again, taking out his pocket watch and handing it to a student in the front row. "Your watches, if you please."

Ezra passed the flesh knives. Mr Lashley dropped one, which fell among the straw on the floor under the operating table. Ezra scrabbled about, picked it up and passed it back. There was a ripple of sound from the crowd. Mr Lashley coughed and set to work.

The woman screamed. She screamed so loud and so high that Mr Lashley stopped cutting. The flesh was in ribbons, half hanging round the bone. Ezra looked at the woman, her face a mask of agony. Shouldn't the man be working faster?

"Someone shut her up!" Lashley hissed, and one of the porters took a pad of leather from his pocket and made the girl bite down on it. "Thank God!" Mr Lashley went back to work. Ezra had counted a minute and a half gone already – but the bone was not exposed cleanly, and he had left no flap of skin to close over the stump.

"Artery hook, sir?" Ezra said, keeping his voice calm and low. Mr Lashley needed to cauterize the femoral artery. Right now.

"Can't you see I'm busy?" Lashley snapped.

From outside Ezra could hear the baby yelling louder than ever.

It was another thirty seconds before the surgeon was ready for the artery hook. The woman's eyes were round in agony. Her face was wet with tears.

"Bone saw!" Lashley barked.

Ezra passed it over and Mr Lashley began sawing. Time seemed to have slowed into eternity. Another minute and a half and he was through; the ruined stump dropped to the floor.

At last the woman faded into unconsciousness.

Ezra looked from the surgeon to the stump. It was not a clean cut. The audience were nudging each other, speaking low; the whole room was thinking the same thing. Ezra had to say something. Surely Mr Lashley couldn't leave it at that?

"What would you have us do, sir?" Ezra asked.

Mr Lashley looked at him with an expression that seemed to be pitched between fury and panic. Then, in a flash, his face changed. He smiled, turned to face the crowd.

"Gentlemen! Scholars! I have decided you shall witness young McAdam's – I mean, McWilliam's – first surgical operation!" He turned back to Ezra and began untying his apron. "Finish up, boy."

"But sir, the cut's not ready to close up."

"I thought I would see how McAdam's boy might do it," Lashley said with a sneer.

Ezra swallowed. "But…"

"No buts. Let's see if you can follow in your master's footsteps."

Ezra stared at him. What was Lashley doing? Of course – he meant to show Ezra up.

He looked at the leg. It was a worse mess than before. And it had been close to four minutes since Lashley had begun his butchery. The woman was now a pale pearly grey, not unlike a fresh cadaver. Ezra felt for a pulse – she was still there, just.

What would the master do? He would have to take some more leg off. If there was a choice between being alive with a shorter stump and dead with a longer one, then there really was no choice at all. But time was running out. The longer an operation took, the less chance the patient had of being alive at the end of it.

Ezra took the bone saw and cut – long, strong, sweeping movements, that's what the master would have said. His heart was pounding, his blood thundering in his ears, but he kept his hands steady – he couldn't afford to waste a second. He cauterized the artery as he'd watched the master do so many times before, then flapped up the skin, careful but quick. Then, as fast as he could, he wadded and bandaged the stump. When he finally let himself wipe his face, he realized he was running with sweat. But he had done it; he had really done it. His first amputation.

That was when he realized the crowd was on its feet,

whistling and cheering. The men in the front row leant forward to shake his hand; there was an avalanche of applause, of *Well done*s, and *Good show*s, and *The old man would be proud*s. Lashley was scowling but Ezra didn't care. He could do this! He could do it well. In fact, Ezra felt at that moment that there was nothing in the whole world he could not have done.

From beyond the noise and celebration of the operating theatre there was still a thin high cry, the woman's baby. Ezra looked back to the table, where a porter was loosing her straps. Another had brought a stretcher, and together they manhandled her onto it like a piece of meat.

"Please! Be careful!" Ezra squeezed back through the crowd. Mr Lashley was there already, looking down at the young woman, a thin smile on his face.

"Take her to the mortuary," he instructed the porters.

"What?" Ezra looked from Lashley to the girl on the stretcher. Her mouth was slack, her eyes staring, open.

"She's dead." Mr Lashley was pleased at last. "No one could survive all that." He looked at Ezra. "You still have a lot to learn, boy." Lashley followed the porters and the body of the dead young woman out of the theatre.

In the hall there was a girl holding the baby, still desperately trying to shush it. She came up to Ezra, her face red and streaked with dirt.

"Oh, sir! Is our Nelly all right? Is she, sir?" she asked.

Ezra felt his mind seize up. He could think of nothing. All the joy and elation he had felt only moments before had vanished. The theatre audience swarmed out past him into the courtyard beyond. Some of them slapped him on his back as they left, told him what a fine fellow he was. One of the students saw the look on his face and told him not to worry. "People die on the table every day, you know that."

He did. He'd seen it many times. But it had never been under his own knife. He wondered when she died exactly. Was it when he cut the bone off, or before? Why hadn't he noticed? Ezra cursed. He should have known better than to try and clean up Lashley's mess.

The girl holding the baby was crying too now, sobbing as the little one screeched. Ezra dug deep in his pockets and pressed the half-shilling he found there into the girl's hand. He was still wearing his apron, stained with blood. What use, he thought, was a surgeon? If someone he cared for – Anna, Mrs Boscaven – got caught in some kind of accident, would he take them to the table, put them through the pain and trauma of an operation? Would it not be kinder to fill them full of gin until they slept and then hold a pillow down hard over their head? Perhaps he should give up now before he killed anyone else.

This was, Ezra was sure, what Lashley had wanted – he was letting the man get to him already! Mr McAdam would never have done that, pitched him in halfway through a procedure. Ezra would not let Mr Lashley's inadequacies as a surgeon ruin his own practice. He would not.

It was grey outside the hospital, the clouds low and dark, and he turned, unconsciously, towards Great Windmill Street – but of course there was only the shut-up shell of a house there now. No Mrs Boscaven making rice pudding, or Ellen to build and light the fire before he woke. Ezra sighed. He had been featherbedded in every sense. He'd had a laboratory and all the books in the world at his disposal, but now... For the past three nights he had shared a tiny garret with Lashley's footman in the man's cold house in Brunswick Square. Ezra imagined that after another few days in those lodgings he might conceivably even miss Toms.

He hadn't seen Loveday Finch since the night in the graveyard and she had sent no message. But she could find where he was simply enough if she wanted to. Those things he'd taken out of her father's head... He closed his eyes and tried to shake the memory away.

Grave-robbing – Anna would think him a prize idiot for agreeing to anything so low. How he would have loved to talk to her now. He tried to imagine sitting down next to her on the bench in the churchyard at St Anne's and explaining all that had happened – four murders in such a short period of time, all of them somehow bound up with a mysterious boy who claimed to be a prince. About Dr McAdam selling the museum and the house, selling him – as good as – to Mr Lashley. About the politics and the Ottoman prince – she would never have believed that. About losing the girl on the operating table... He sighed. Anna would tell him to go back and bear it, work through it. She would have said the girl's death was God's will, that no man could have changed a thing. Ezra smiled. He should have liked to see Anna in argument with Monsieur Bichat and his kind, those who saw surgery in the future able to extend knowledge, perhaps extend life, in ways they could only dream of. And Ezra knew he wanted to be a part of that – whatever else happened on the way.

The surgery had been a mistake, he said to himself,

and next time he would make sure things were different. Better. Ezra found himself back outside the hospital and went inside, he had work to do. He began to change the blood- and bone-spattered straw that lay on the floor of the theatre. Then he sat close to the brazier and ate his lunch of bread and cheese that had been wrapped up in his apron pocket all morning. He rested his feet on the edge of the stove and enjoyed the feeling of the heat seeping up through the soles of his boots. He drifted off into sleep for a moment. In his dream the baby cried and the girl was dead on the table. Then his boots slid off the brazier and landed with a thump on the floor, jolting him awake.

At that moment the theatre doors swung open and the small figure of Miss Loveday Finch, wearing a black floor-length cloak and a black bonnet, swept in.

"Mr McAdam, I have found you at last!" She was out of breath, her grey eyes shone. "I have so much to say. We are so close to making sense of *everything*!"

"Then truly I am glad for you."

"Don't mock me! It was just as I said: the boy was the key. I have written it all down, everything he said, everything that happened in Constantinople, and everything that was in father's letter."

"You had it translated?" Ezra sat up.

"Yes, by a very kind young man at the Algerian coffee shop on Swallow Street. His name was George. I had to promise to teach him how to turn a red handkerchief blue."

"How can you trust him?"

"He had kind eyes, and he said my hair was beautiful. I trust him as much as I trusted you, anyway. And I copied out a translation – which took me a whole candle – and sent it to Great Windmill Street, but you were not there."

"No." Ezra looked away.

"But listen –" Loveday ploughed on regardless – "I have great news! Important news. And you must come with me. Now!"

Ezra thought later that if he had been wide awake he would have argued with her, but still on the edge of sleep he merely jumped up, brushed the crumbs from his lap and let her help him off with his apron and pull him out into the street.

"Where are we going?" he asked. "I have to be back for the afternoon lecture. And you must refrain from calling me McAdam – Dr James has waved a hand and made it so, apparently."

"What should I call you, then?" she asked.

"Ezra will do well enough. After this morning I am not sure I deserve any surname at all."

"Don't be such a misery," Miss Finch said and sped up, running in between the traffic on Ludgate Hill and by St Paul's Cathedral. She was right. He bit his tongue, but then another thought made him pull her to a stop, just by the junction with Fleet Street. "Miss Finch, please."

"Call me Loveday." She stopped and turned to face him. "I think you know me well enough by now."

"Where are we going?" He lowered his voice. "Because if it is to dig up yet another body, I will not be part of this enterprise."

"Do you think me quite mad?" she exclaimed.

"Sometimes, yes, I think I do!" The two of them

stared at each other, stubbornly, at the side of the road. "Whatever you might have found," he said, "there is no point any more. I am in no mood."

She rolled her eyes. "So change your mood, sir, and come along."

"I am not an automaton!" He raised his voice to be heard above the traffic. "I killed a young woman on the table this morning. I have never done that, yet." He paused. "You cannot know what that is like."

"Perhaps not. But you deal with life and death every day, and I don't doubt, if the poor girl was on your table, that you were her very last hope."

The traffic swirled east and west and north and south. Cries for apples and pears, nuts and hot pies rang out around them.

Loveday said, more gently this time, "If you want to be a good surgeon, this will happen again – is that not so?"

"Of course."

"So I am taking your mind off one worry and asking you to replace it with another. Is that so bad?" She grinned at him. "I have found out something, which, in the run of things, may greatly improve your situation, and, in doing so, improve mine own." She took her bag from under her cloak and pulled something out.

"This is the lead shot that killed your master," she declared triumphantly. "There are some advantages – only a few, mind – to being a girl. I sweet-talked the coroner into letting me see it and palmed it while he was too afraid or surprised to quarrel with me. I am not sure which."

Ezra tried to speak but she went on.

"I am certain that you could prove it is of a piece with

the shot that killed our tongueless friend, whose name, Mahmoud tells me, was Abd." She passed it to him and he felt the weight of it drop into his hand. "From Mr Ahmat's gun, no doubt."

"This little thing is the cause of all of my misfortune?" Ezra turned it over in his hand.

"Oh no," Loveday said. "I think you will find your misfortune rests just as heavily on the shoulders of Dr James McAdam of Edinburgh, or your Mr Lashley."

"He is not mine, I assure you," Ezra said, turning the lead pellet over in his hand and marvelling that such a small thing could do so much damage. "But how do you expect me to be able to prove that this comes from the same gun as the shot that killed the tongueless cadaver? That pellet is boxed up with the museum collection. Even if I could locate it, I have no laboratory to work in; the ones at the hospital are next to useless."

"Aha!" Loveday took the lead pellet back and snapped it into her bag. "That's exactly what I thought. You need to get back to Great Windmill Street, the proof is there. If we could get at the truth of your master's will and find for certain what he left you it would help, wouldn't it?" She took Ezra's hand and led him through the arch into the Middle Temple. "Here!" She spread her arms. "More lawyers than bedbugs in a sailors' boarding house! More importantly, your master's lawyer, Mr Robert Harkaway. I have been talking to Franny, his maid of all work, who lights the fires and brings her lawyer master hot tea and sees all. You cannot give up, Ezra – *we* cannot – not now! Would your Mr McAdam have wanted that?"

Ezra shook his head, reeling from all she had told him.

Perhaps there was something to be said for the irrepressible Miss Loveday Finch after all.

The sun squeezed through the winter cloud as they came through the arch into the Fountain Court of the Middle Temple. Neither of them looked out of place in their mourning blacks as the lawyers and lawyers' clerks scurried between buildings carrying bundles of paper tied in bright pinkish-red tape.

"Miss Finch…"

She made a face at him.

"Loveday, then," Ezra sighed. "What do you imagine this lawyer will do? Show us Mr McAdam's will?"

"Well, we won't know until we ask him, will we?" She led him up some steps and knocked on a black painted door.

A young man opened it and told them Mr Harkaway was busy. "Tell him Mr Ezra McAdam is here to see him," Loveday instructed. "Tell him that we will wait." Ezra followed her inside.

"My name is McWilliam now," Ezra hissed, but Loveday shushed him.

"It was your name, and you should have kept it. If I were you I would have done."

"I did not fancy my chances facing Dr James in court," said Ezra.

"I would cut him down," Loveday whispered back.

Ezra almost smiled. "There are subtleties to life, Miss Finch!"

"With some people," she retorted, "and I don't doubt your Dr James is one of them, subtlety gets you absolutely nowhere."

Inside, the office was unbearably hot. Ezra took off his overcoat but Loveday kept her cloak on, and Ezra could see her face was rapidly turning almost as red as her hair.

He was about to suggest she removed it when the clerk came back.

"Mr Harkaway will see you now."

The lawyer's office was just as warm, and painted all over brown, so it felt rather like entering the den of a small animal – appropriately so, because when Mr Harkaway looked up Ezra thought he resembled nothing so much as a badger given human form.

"Mr McAdam?"

Ezra leant forward, his hand out to shake the lawyer's, but Mr Harkaway merely stopped writing and looked first Loveday and then Ezra up and down.

"Is this concerning Mr William McAdam? You are family?"

"Yes and no."

"Which is it, boy? I am busy."

"Mr McAdam was my master, sir," Ezra ventured, "and your client. I believe he made a will."

"Indeed." Mr Harkaway nodded.

"We don't believe it was read," Ezra said.

"Or referred to," Loveday added.

Mr Harkaway sat up. "So you are not family, then."

"No," said Ezra uncertainly.

"He was as good as! The master was like his father," Loveday put in. "Might have adopted him."

Ezra nudged her to shut her up.

"*Like* and *was* are two unrelated words," Mr Harkaway said, "just as you and Mr McAdam are not related. And so I am unable, by law, to show you the will."

"Please, sir! Is there no way…?"

"There is no way. Good day to you both."

"How can we see it, then? Tell us that?" Ezra tried not to sound desperate.

The man's tone had become frosty. "I said, good day."

Loveday suddenly opened her cloak and took out the rapier that was hanging at her waist.

"What on earth are you doing, Loveday?" cried Ezra. "Put it away!"

"Crean! Help, Crean!" Harkaway was calling for his clerk, who bustled in. "These two are mad! A girl with a sword and a mulatto with a scar. Call the watch, Crean. Call the watch!"

Ezra put his hand firmly on the blade. "No need, Mr Harkaway. I am sorry for my companion." He shot Loveday a look. "We are leaving. Now."

Ezra took the blade and bundled her out into the Fountain Court.

"I don't know what you think you were doing!" he hissed.

"I was helping! I was getting him to show us the will! Give me my blade back."

"No! You could have had us locked up. Again!" Ezra paused to try and calm himself. "I think, Miss Finch, you read too many novels. One doesn't go barging into law-yers' offices with a sword."

"A duelling rapier. My father's," corrected Loveday, who was not chastised in the least. "And how else do you think I got the coroner to show me the shot that killed your master?"

"You threatened him, too?"

"Only a little."

Ezra fumed. "I am going back to St Bartholomew's," he informed her. "I have a position with Lashley – just. I may not like it, but he gives me a bed to sleep in. I will not have you lose my only security chasing a dream." He began to walk away.

"All I have now is dreams!" Loveday called after him. "Wait till you read the letter! It is all there!" Ezra kept walking. She shouted again, "And you have my duelling piece!"

Ezra turned back. He handed her the rapier carefully, by the handle. It had begun to rain, the drops so cold and hard they almost felt like hail.

"Miss Finch," he said, "I have lost my master and my home. I have no doubt that the Ottoman Empire is somehow responsible, although heaven knows what your father was doing acting as some kind of courier for precious jewels. But you and I, we are powerless. People have died – this is not a game! I do not see that one person armed with her father's duelling rapier could possibly do a thing about it, and I will not be involved in illegalities of any kind ever again!" Ezra felt himself shaking with rage. The girl was an idiot. "Don't you realize the consequences if we are caught? Do you know what we just did?"

Ezra turned away. He could not look at her any more. He wanted his old life back, a life where Mrs Boscaven brewed hot coffee and the master made him shred the veins from skin while barking Greek verbs at him all night. Loveday Finch blinked at him. She had no idea at all.

"I have had enough, Miss Finch. You can keep your money." His words fell as hard and cold as the rain. "Hear this: I do not wish to see you, or hear a word about your plots and schemes, ever again."

Chapter Thirteen

Mr Leonard Lashley's Residence
Brunswick Square
Bloomsbury
London
November 1792

Ezra lay in his bed shivering. It was so cold that ice had formed on the inside of the window. He had been at Lashley's only one week but it seemed like a hundred years. On the bed closest to the fire, Evans, the footman, snored loudly.

Ezra rolled himself tighter in his blankets, shut his eyes again and prayed he would sleep. He had too many thoughts swirling around his head. He wondered if there was a nerve, like an artery that supplied the brain with blood, perhaps – that maybe he had over-stimulated it with too much thinking. Even though he'd sworn to have nothing more to do with Miss Loveday Finch, even though he had spent the last four days doing his best to keep her from his mind, he couldn't help thinking that if she was right, someone needed to act. He had never come across a girl so rash. It must be the theatrical background.

He breathed hot moist air into his cupped hands to

warm them. Anna would have told him to keep his head down and work hard; that, in time, things would work themselves out, including – though he was beginning to doubt it – Mr McAdam's will. But even if the will was found, he would hardly have his place at Great Windmill Street back, not if the house was sold.

Anna, sensible and rational in all things, would say it didn't matter. She would tell him he was the same person whatever name he wore. He tried to call her face to mind, her long hair, her brown eyes, but it wouldn't come. He was forgetting her… Did that mean she was forgetting him?

He missed their long, rational discussions on life and death and religion. He missed *her*. But how on earth would Anna ever find him with a new name and a new home? Loveday had tracked him down at Bart's, but how would Anna do the same from Holland? If she did find a way to write to him, it would be to his old address. Ezra had to inform her – let her know where he was.

He would take his new address to Betsey at the cloth warehouse. That was the least he could do, then when Anna came looking for him she would know where he was. He sat up, pulling the blankets with him.

It was still dark, half past five, but if he left now he would get back to Bart's in time to ready the operating theatre for another of Mr Lashley's woeful lectures.

Ezra dressed and made it to Soho before the church clock had begun to strike six. Perhaps it was still much too early. He looked up at the shuttered cloth warehouse – no sign of Betsey. He left a note and decided to make a quick detour to Great Windmill Street. He promised himself he would only stop a moment. Just to look.

Ezra passed the bakery on the corner where Archer Street met Rupert Street and he greeted the baker's boy, who, pleased to see a friendly face again, sold him a hot tuppenny loaf for a penny. Ezra held it close and tore bits off as he walked, popping the hot bread into his mouth and savouring the warm, soft deliciousness that tasted of home.

As he turned into Great Windmill Street he heard Mrs Perino's cockerel, and he knew this had been a bad idea. He felt such a longing, not only for Mr McAdam, but for his old life, that his throat felt tight, and there was a feeling in his chest as if someone had punched a hole in his sternum and plucked out his heart.

Ezra looked through the letter flap. The hall was empty. Letters piled up like a miniature snowdrift. Who knew what might be there? Oh, there would be Loveday's letter – the one that, if she were here, she would defend as containing the answers to absolutely everything. But perhaps there was something else there, maybe even something from Anna. He sighed. The door was locked. He looked through the basement window into the lifeless kitchen below – perhaps he could get in there? At that moment a cart trundled down the street, and Ezra stepped back. Someone might see. He would to all intents and purposes appear as any common ken cracker. He had to be careful.

He broke off another piece of bread, went around the back of the house to Ham Yard and helped himself to a drink at the water pump. He wanted that post – he just had to find a way in. Ezra looked at the glass-roofed lecture theatre, especially built, the most up to date in

London, now empty and unused. What a waste.

Then he noticed the door. It seemed jammed into place rather than snugly closed. Something was wrong – had someone broken in already?

Even in the early morning half-light he was sure of it. He pressed the handle, but it was still bolted from the inside. Then he realized one of the panels had been knocked out and replaced – it moved easily, and Ezra reached in and slid the bolt. The door opened.

The floor was swept clean, the benches piled up against one wall. The dark wooden table, the one the master had had made specially, was still in place in the centre of the room. Ezra checked the yard – no one was looking. He stepped inside.

He ran his hand along the table and shut his eyes. He imagined himself here less than a month ago, assisting the master, the room packed with students. A sound from the main house jolted him out of his dream. Was someone in there? He tried the door that led through to the hallway and it opened easily.

"Who's there?" Ezra shouted up into the house. No reply. It was probably no more than a pigeon flapping in through an open window, he told himself. He should leave, get back to the cloth warehouse and go to work. After he had collected his post.

In the hall, the large oval mirror was still turned, mourning wise, to face the wall. He turned it back and regarded himself, then took up the post and went into the master's office to sift through it. A thought struck him as he took in the shuttered windows, the master's chair covered with a dust sheet and another over his desk. Dr

James's wish to clear the house of furniture as quickly as possible had obviously not been met. Ezra smiled. He was glad to think that the man hadn't had everything his own way.

Most of the post was for Dr James or the master. There was nothing from Anna, but he recognized Loveday's letter straight away, untidy, like its sender, almost bursting open. He couldn't bring himself to sit at the master's desk, but he leant against the wall and was about to start reading when a noise came from upstairs, from the museum. A definite creak, and not a pigeon or a rat; it was too loud. Ezra put the letter down and listened – there, again. He stepped back into the hall and took the stairs two at a time, bursting through into the museum, empty now except for a few chests of drawers.

The door to his own bedroom at the far end moved almost imperceptibly. Ezra looked round. He had no weapon and there was nothing to hand.

Perhaps if he went down to look in the kitchen? No! Whoever it was might have gone by then. He stuffed the remains of the loaf in his jacket pocket and made his way down the length of what had been the museum. Ezra knew every floorboard, which creaked and which didn't; he made it to his bedroom door in silence.

Gingerly, he pushed it open. Inside, the curtains were drawn but there was a small fire in the hearth and, balanced on top, Mrs Boscaven's kettle.

"What the devil...?"

But he could see no one. The bed was obviously being slept in, an untidy mess of blankets and rugs piled in a heap, but there was not a soul in sight. At the same moment that Ezra realized whoever it was must be behind the door, it was pushed hard into his face. He staggered backwards in pain, then righted himself, lifted the poker and readied to strike, imagining Oleg, the man who'd wrecked the museum and who, as far as Ezra knew, was still at large.

A voice rang out, "Stop!"

"You!" Ezra cried. The boy, Mahmoud, the prince of wherever, looking distinctly less prince-like even than that night in the graveyard. "In my room! In my bed!"

"I am sorry. I had not meant to hurt you."

Ezra sat down, rubbing his forehead where the door had smashed into it.

"I cannot be too careful, and I was doing no harm. There was no one here. No one at all," he said in his strange imperious tone. He was staring longingly at the half a loaf that was stuck, crust side down, into Ezra's pocket.

Ezra took it out and held it up. "You may have this, on account that you tell me what you are doing in my bed."

The boy nodded and fell upon the loaf as if he were a wolf and it were a lamb.

Perhaps Ezra was dreaming. He would not have put it past Miss Loveday Finch to have staged this charade for her own amusement. He looked around his old room, half expecting her to jump out from under the bed.

"I am here because I know your house and it was empty," said Mahmoud. As he spoke he picked at any crumbs that had fallen onto the bed. "There is no other reason. I could not go back to school, and I have not yet endeavoured to exchange the stones for currency. As soon as that is done I will leave this city. But at present

I must admit I am afraid to go out. Nowhere is safe for me any more."

"Does Loved— does Miss Finch know you are here?"

"I think it is better that she does not. It is too dangerous," said Mahmoud, looking momentarily nervous. "In any case it is none of her business."

"Not her business!" Ezra stared at him in frustration. "She risked a spell in a lock-up for you, as did I!"

"It would not have helped anyone if I had stayed around and got myself caught. And, as I see, you escaped." The boy shrugged. "So no harm was done."

Ezra thought him completely self-regarding.

"You are spoilt and ill mannered. She has only tried to help you, to find out who killed her father and why."

"You do not understand, Mr Ezra McAdam. That is your name, I think?" Mahmoud spoke as if he sat cross-legged on a silk cushion in fine robes, not on the floor of an unheated bedroom of an empty house in London; as if he were a grown man, not a young boy. "There are forces moving against me here in this city. I do not wish to see any more die." He nodded. "You have both done me good turns and the house of Othman thanks you – because of you they think I am dead; they think I am the boy you anatomized."

"So *that's* it!" The gunman's questions began to make sense. No wonder he had been more interested in the drowned boy than the tongueless man. "*They?* Do you mean Mr Ahmat? Is he your countryman?"

"I do not know anyone by that name."

"Mr Ahmat. The man who killed my master, Mr McAdam. He works at the embassy, it was reported in

The Times. I believe he also shot the man with no tongue," Ezra added.

At this, Mahmoud looked daggers at him. "The man's name was Abd. I had known him since I was a child. He was a good friend."

"Friend? I hardly think the removal of a tongue—"

Mahmoud interrupted. "He had no tongue because of some slight that occurred in his youth. It should not have happened. If I were sultan…"

He wiped his eye; he looked suddenly vulnerable. "Abd was my bodyguard." Mahmoud coughed, sat up straight and was a prince again. He went on. "And I can tell you the name of Abd's killer. I was there, in hiding when the toad's mother who calls himself a friend of the empire despatched him. Abd who was nothing but good. Abd who was kind…"

"Who was it, then? Is he still here in London, at the embassy?"

"I do not care what happens to that snake in human form. God will punish him, in this life or the next."

"Mahmoud, listen. You're quite sure you don't know an Ahmat? Tall fellow, pointed beard?"

"Not Ahmat, no. But Abd's killer was tall and bearded. Well dressed."

"I swear it's the same man!" Ezra sat up.

Mahmoud spat into the fire. "There is more than one source of evil in this world. Abd went to fetch the rubies. For me. Instead poor Abd met his death. He will be at peace now."

"And you have no wish for justice?" Ezra leant forward, curious.

Mahmoud smiled. "You are a clever man. Miss Finch told me all about you. A doctor of some kind, she said." Ezra nodded. Mahmoud continued, "You know the path the blood takes around the body. You know how the heart works, how the sinews under our skin move and flex. But you do not understand that in this world, on this earth, there is no such thing as justice?"

"I don't believe that," Ezra declared. "I don't believe that we should take our lot and struggle on to gain – what? – our reward once we are dead. This world should be fair. No kings, no emperors."

"No sultans?" Mahmoud smirked.

"No sultans." Ezra tried not to get angry. "Mahmoud, I was born a slave."

Mahmoud nodded. "Slaves are a fact of life. Abd, he was a good slave."

"No! I do not believe that. Who says which man is a slave?"

"God, of course. Don't Christians believe that too?"

"I don't. No one man should belong to another. No man should have that power. That is wrong." Ezra scowled. He got up and riddled the fire with the poker. "I care who killed Mr McAdam. My life has been thrown into chaos because of your stupid empire."

"The Empire is not stupid!" Mahmoud squared up to Ezra, fists up.

Ezra looked at him, a scrap of humanity dancing back and forth in front of the fire, filthy as a night soil man, his fists on a level with Ezra's shoulder. He was a little boy in danger, far from home. Ezra knew that feeling. He sighed.

"Mahmoud, we should not fight, you and I. I apologize for slighting the Ottoman Empire. But I promise I will bring Mr McAdam's killer to justice. And Abd's, too."

The prince sat down slowly. Ezra sat down next to him. The light of the flames glowed on the boy's pale face.

"Do you think Abd knew his killer? Did he tell you who he was meeting?" Ezra asked. "Well, obviously, not with words…"

Mahmoud hugged his knees. "Abd used the language that our servants use at court. Though not so much these days."

"The servants have their own language?"

"Yes, Ixarette. It enables you to speak without words, without sounds. The sultan does not like to be disturbed, so the servants speak with their hands, see?" Mahmoud spelt out what Ezra imagined were words with his fingers in the air. He sighed. "I have had enough of this place," he said, pulling his knees closer to his chest, and for once he seemed his age. "I want to go home."

"I see that," Ezra murmured. "Back to everything you know."

The boy looked at him, blinked. "Yes, that is it." He nodded. "Exactly."

The church at St Anne's struck for seven, and Ezra stood up. He had to be at Bart's in half an hour.

"Well," he said gently, "I'd like nothing more than to go back to my home, too, but that's impossible. What's more, I have a job of work. I am sorry, you will have to excuse me."

"You won't tell anyone I am here?" the boy said.

"Please?" He looked at Ezra. His eyes were glistening.

Ezra promised he wouldn't, then paused at the door, watching for a moment as Mahmoud pulled his rags about his feet. He was just a boy, alone in a city with no family and no friends.

Ezra searched in Mrs Boscaven's linen cupboard and found an old blanket. He took it back down to Mahmoud but he was already deep asleep. Ezra carefully and quietly tucked the boy in and slipped away.

As soon as Ezra turned towards Holborn he could feel the cold working its way into his bones. He remembered one Christmas Mrs Boscaven had knitted him a pair of gloves. He shoved his hands deep into his coat pockets and felt something. A packet? He pulled it out. Loveday's letter.

By the time he'd reached St Giles Ezra had walked into a laundrywoman and two hot pie sellers, who'd all cursed him in a variety of different accents.

"Watch your step, lad!" a carter yelled as he stepped out into the road.

He did not notice.

For Miss Finch's letter was riveting – far more gripping than one of the latest Gothic novels, and just as far-fetched.

Ezra arrived at St Bartholomew's out of breath, running with sweat and half an hour late. Mr Lashley was waiting, apron on, regarding the morning's cadaver as if it were a piece of mutton that was too stringy for the pot – poking it in the thigh, the arm, the stomach. Ezra swallowed. He looked at the thing that had been a man and silently apologized to it on Mr Lashley's behalf.

"You are late! The body is here and you are not! Perhaps I should divest you of your apprenticeship and give it to this chap here." He picked up the cadaver's right arm and waved it. "I'd be your apprentice in a trice, Mr Lashley!" He made the cadaver speak in a stupid, high-pitched voice. "And I'd never be late or kill your patients when they came to me for help, oh no!"

Ezra kept his eyes on the floor. He wondered how a grown man could amuse himself like a novice medical student, but he said only, "Sorry, sir."

"You had better be!" Lashley said. "Students are here. Chop chop, apron on, instruments in order. Now!"

Ezra checked and lined up his master's old knives while the students filed in and sat down. His mind was not on them, though. He was imagining telling the master everything that Loveday had written in her letter: how she had discovered her father was acting as a courier for the valide sultan, how she had found the name of the bank account Mr Finch had opened under a false name in order to deposit the fee for carrying the rubies – and how the letter from her father to Mr Falcon, who knew nothing of the scheme, had contained an apology for keeping it secret from him. Loveday had found out that her father had been worried someone was following them even before they'd left Turkey, and she had deduced the performance at the embassy was to be when the jewels were to be handed over to Abd, the tongueless man, to take to Mahmoud. But Abd had never turned up, and Mr Finch had been murdered. Someone at the embassy was clearly acting with the Russians. And Loveday wrote that she had seen the reports in the newspapers: Ahmat was in prison awaiting trial, locked up and, no doubt, heading for the hangman. But, Loveday warned, there had to be someone else, still working at the embassy, still set on overthrowing the sultan and deposing Mahmoud's family. Loveday wrote that she was certain she was being followed.

A few weeks ago Ezra would have dismissed such ideas as fanciful. But now, with an Ottoman prince in hiding in an empty house, he suspected she was telling the truth.

Meanwhile, Loveday proposed finding out exactly who was following her. Her plan, which involved breaking into the embassy, was as outlandish and colourful as her hair. Ezra remembered the last time they'd tried to get in – it was impossible. But Loveday had no comprehension of the word. Ezra smiled thinking about it.

"Boy! The number two flesh knife!" Lashley barked.

Ezra jolted out of his reverie. He was at work. On the anatomizing table the corpse lay open like a strange flower.

"And why in heaven's name are you grinning like an idiot?"

Ezra passed the knife but missed Lashley's hand. The knife clattered onto the floor, singing off the straw-covered stone flags and echoing around the lecture theatre.

Ezra quickly retrieved it. "Mr Lashley," he said quietly, "I think you'll find the master used this knife for removing the lungs and heart, not—"

"If you would keep your comments to yourself, boy." Lashley turned back to the cadaver, and Ezra winced as the surgeon butchered the lungs and then the heart, tearing one of the ventricles open as he tried to remove it in one piece.

There was some sniggering at the back of the class. Ezra put the heart into a dish while Mr Lashley pointed out the main arteries.

"Ezra, prepare the heart to show the chambers," Lashley ordered.

"I'm afraid I can't, sir. It's not intact – the right ventricle…"

Ezra could hear some more laughing.

Lashley was getting angry, and his voice was rising. "I said, don't argue with me, boy!"

"But…"

Someone in the crowd called out, "I say, what a mess."

"That's it!" Lashley yelled. "Lecture over. All of you, OUT!" He turned to Ezra. "And you! You might have forgotten, but I am your master now."

"I am sorry, sir. I was simply—"

"Simply nothing! You are too damned clever for your own good. You think you know everything but you are a boy. You hear me? A boy! I should sell you to the West Indies, then you would know hard work. You can leave this post and you can leave my house. If there are any of your possessions left here, know this: I will burn them all."

There was silence. It was as if the whole room was holding its breath.

Ezra picked up the flesh knife, wiped it carefully and put it back in its place on the instrument table, in order. His hand was shaking. "Mr Lashley," he said coolly, "thank you for letting me go. Working for you has made these last few weeks since Mr McAdam's death intolerable. Sir, I pity your students, but more than that I pity your patients." Ezra turned to the medical students, none of whom had moved from their seats. The silence was so thick you could have cut it with one of the knives lined up neatly on the bench.

He addressed the room. "I would advise any medical student who wishes to advance their knowledge of human anatomy to get to a better school and a better teacher than this."

As he took off his apron the silence broke in a wave of applause. The students were on their feet, stamping, clapping. Through the tumultuous noise, Ezra could even make out some *Bravo*s and a couple of *Hear, hear*s.

Lashley's face was redder than the chest cavity of the open cadaver.

His heart pounding heavily in his own chest, Ezra hung up his apron and put on his jacket. Then he swung out through the theatre doors and into the courtyard of St Bartholomew's.

The sky was clear and the sounds of the cattle in the market at Smithfield sounded almost pastoral. Ezra thought on Mr Lashley, furious as an ox about to enter the abattoir, and felt much better than he had in a very long time.

Chapter Fourteen

Coldbath Fields House of Correction
Coldbath Fields
Clerkenwell
London
November 1792

Ezra stood in front of the prison gates and rang the bell. Behind the crumbling red brick wall he could hear the inmates, and the sounds did nothing to change his opinion that the dead were often infinitely less terrifying than the living.

He had cleared out of Brunswick Square in minutes. He had few possessions apart from the clothes he stood up in and his leather apron, which he'd rolled up and carried over his shoulder. Earlier this morning he had also owned a good coat and an illustrated book on anatomy the master had presented to him last Christmas, but he had pawned both in exchange for the three silver coins he now turned over and over in his pocket, where they rested against the pages of Miss Finch's letter.

Ezra wished he hadn't yelled at her and told her he wanted nothing to do with her again. Her theories were outrageous, but, together with everything he'd seen and what Mahmoud had told him, they all made sense. He'd wasted time playing the good apprentice in Lashley's service when he should have attended Mr Falcon's post-mortem. He would have bet his three silver coins that Mr Falcon's heart would have looked as shrivelled as Mr Finch's.

After the trip to the pawnbroker Ezra had gone to the magistrate's office in the hope of explaining that Mr Ahmat, who had shot his master, was also responsible for the deaths of two conjurors and was in fact part of something bigger. He had been laughed out of the office.

Ezra recalled the faces of the gunman and his accomplice and cursed. He needed proof; he needed to be certain that whoever was responsible for Abd's death had also had Mr Finch and Mr Falcon poisoned. Was Ahmat acting alone? There was one way to find out, Ezra had decided: go straight to the source, talk to Ahmat in person. After all, he was in prison now, safely locked up, awaiting the hangman. Ezra wasn't foolish enough to think he would tell all, but perhaps he could get the man to give something away.

After a long wait, a tall man, rather in need of a good shave, shuffled out of the gatehouse. Ezra hesitated. This could not be as bad as the Fortune of War, he told himself, and stepped forward.

"Excuse me, sir!'

The man squinted at him. "Don't I know you?" he said. "I do, I do! That scar." He pointed at Ezra's face. "I'd remember a phiz like that any day of the week. You's that surgeon's boy, ain't you? Best thing my wife ever done for me, get me a ticket to one of his lectures." The man whistled, remembering. "Damnedest thing, to see inside a body, how it works, all blood an' bones! You are him, ain't you? Bad news your master's death was – well, we got the cove that done it, that we did."

"Yes—"

The man cut in. "Don't tell me." He began to turn the lock and open the gate. "That's why you're here, to see the man what done your master in." He waved Ezra in. "The pleasure," he said, "is entirely mine."

Ezra didn't know what to say. He hadn't thought it would be so simple to get in. He followed the warder – "My name's Harries" – round the outside of the crumbling prison walls to a door that led down underneath the mass of the building.

Harries kept on talking as they descended the stone steps, but Ezra wasn't listening. He was too busy going over in his head what to ask, how to approach this – but all his questions went out of his head when Mr Harries opened the door.

There, laid on a table covered in a winding sheet, was a body. It wasn't a cell – it was a mortuary.

"We did for him this morning," the warder said.

"He's dead!" Ezra exclaimed. "But there was no trial! I was never called as witness…"

"I hear as he confessed – well, not with words, exactly, of course. Signed something, he did. And there's no point them keep taking up space when they're guilty." Harries began to unwind the sheet. "There you go – and if you, you know, want to do a bit of anatomizing on him now, like, feel free. The bugger deserves everything he gets."

The face of the hanged man on the table was bloated,

its eyes bulging. A thick red rope burn ran under its chin and around the neck.

But it wasn't the man who'd killed the master.

"Was this the man called Ahmat? You are sure?" Ezra said at last.

"Oh yes. The Turks what brought him in told the magistrate so. The fella couldn't speak a word of English," Harries said, smiling. "In fact, he didn't say much at all – look."

Harries opened the man's mouth. It was a mess, a bloody pulpy mess – he'd had his tongue cut out, but it must have been recently.

This short, square man had nothing in common with the slight, narrow-faced gunman who had called himself Ahmat – or his towering accomplice, for that matter. Ezra stepped forward, unravelled the sheet further and pulled out the man's right arm. Perhaps he would have a tattoo like Abd; perhaps this was some poor sod who worked for the harem or the embassy – but there was nothing there. On his left arm was a sailor's tattoo, as he'd seen on many cadavers washed up in the Thames.

Ezra checked the body over completely. As well as the removal of the tongue, the man had suffered a blow to the head, possibly at or around the same time.

Whoever did this had probably got some poor drink-sotten cove out of a tavern, coshed him, cut out his tongue so he couldn't speak and given him to the magistrates as Ahmat.

"The fellows that turned him in, do you know who they were?" Ezra asked.

Harries shrugged. "Grand, I can tell you that – from

the embassy, I heard. Turned in one of their own, they did, on account of how he did in poor Mr McAdam, the best surgeon in London."

Ezra nodded to Harries. "Thank you." He handed him one of the silver pieces. The warder looked disappointed that he wasn't going to get to see any anatomizing, but Ezra was sure this body would have nothing to show him. Besides, he had no time to waste – Mr Ahmat was still out in the city, and by the sound of it safe in the embassy. Mahmoud was not safe.

Coldbath Fields was less than a quarter-mile from Clerkenwell Green. Ezra covered the distance in minutes, and knocked hard on the door of Mrs Gurney's townhouse.

No one came. He knocked again. This time the maid opened the door, the look on her face one of irritation.

"They are all out!" She began to close the door.

"No, wait. Perhaps you could take a message? For Miss Finch?"

The maid shook her head. "Miss Finch has left."

"Left?" Ezra felt fear grip his heart. Had Ahmat come for her already? "When? Is she still in London?"

"Mrs Gurney said that some gentlemen come looking for her and she did a flit. Left her rent, though, she did."

"What men? Do you know what they looked like?"

The maid rolled her eyes. "I said as it wasn't me. If you want to take it up with Mrs Gurney…"

"No, no." Ezra stepped back and the door shut hard. He looked around. What if something had already happened to Loveday? Why had he been such a petulant idiot and walked away?

Ezra kicked a stone out into the road. He liked to

think of himself like the young French surgeons, rational, sober, but sometimes he could be as much a creature of wilfulness as Miss Finch.

Ezra had reached Holborn before he realized he had no idea where he was going. He wasn't thinking; his mind was fogged up with worry and something else. Dread. He scanned every face on the street, terrified he'd walk into Oleg or Ahmat. He had to find somewhere safe. The city was a blur of people and movement – where could he go? There was only one answer, the only place that had ever been home: Great Windmill Street.

Ezra made his way in through Ham Yard as he had done early that morning. He was careful to make sure no one was watching as he slipped inside the lecture room and then into the house. He called out to Mahmoud, who appeared at the top of the stairs looking cleaner and better dressed than earlier, clutching a whole pie in one hand. He was smiling, too.

"Miss Finch is here. We have been waiting for you all day."

Loveday appeared next to Mahmoud on the landing and Ezra felt the tension in his bones ebb away.

"Thank heavens! I went to the house – the maid told me some men—"

"I thought they might come after me. So I am wearing my travelling habit. She lifted up the skirts of her dress and they positively clanked. She grinned. "I remember Pa saying it's always best to carry money close. I suppose he was talking about the rubies, too. Come in, there's dinner."

Ezra followed them into the master's office to find a picnic laid out on one of the dust sheets.

Mahmoud sat down cross-legged on the floor, finished his pie and took another. He and Loveday assured Ezra that this was the Turkish fashion and so most apt.

Ezra watched them share a joke about a dog, a fox and a three-legged milking stool, and he wished he could be that easy with people, especially when lives were in danger.

He went to the window and looked out through a hole in the shutter. Out in the street, life went on as normal. Assassins were only notable by their absence.

"What is up with you, Ezra McWhatsit?" Loveday said, brushing the crumbs off her dress. "Mahmoud and I have put the world to rights while you look out of the window with a face as long as Friday."

"Sorry, I was distracted," Ezra said. "I was thinking how there can never be justice in this whole matter. I saw the man they hanged today for my master's murder – the man they think is Ahmat – and it was not him. That means we are still in danger."

Mahmoud wiped his mouth. "I would simply tell the magistrates they have made a mistake."

Ezra sighed. "They laughed me out of their offices. I am just a surgeon's apprentice. No one would believe me."

"The word of a servant is never worth as much as that of a man of substance," said Mahmoud. "That is the way of things."

Ezra scowled. Loveday gave him a sharp look and unwrapped a parcel of three small seed cakes.

"Cake, see?"

But Ezra was not to be distracted. "Mahmoud, you may

not care who lives or dies, but I guarantee this Ahmat and his Russian friend are working to unpick your beloved empire."

Mahmoud nodded slowly. "This Ahmat is a dog. Perhaps if I could see the ambassador himself…"

"Surely he would believe *you*," Loveday said. "The son of the sultan."

"I am not supposed to be here," Mahmoud reminded her. "He would call me an impostor. It would go badly for my grandmother, too, if I was found out."

They were all quiet for a long while. Mahmoud ate up every last crumb until the dust sheet was perfectly and completely clean. Loveday ruffled his hair as if to apologize for not having any more food, and Ezra saw the street boy again, not the sultan.

Ezra sat up. "There is only one answer. Mahmoud must leave as soon as possible, sell the jewels, use the money and get away before he is hunted down."

"But then your Ahmat would still be at the embassy, dripping poison," said Mahmoud.

Ezra looked at him, surprised, but could see by his thoughtful frown that he was in earnest. It seemed the boy was more willing to take Ahmat seriously when he was considered a threat to his precious empire.

"I know," said Loveday. "We can take a letter signed by you, Mahmoud. We could take it straight to the ambassador."

Ezra looked at her. "We went to the embassy, remember? They wouldn't even let us through the door!"

Mahmoud nodded at Loveday. "Yes. You must find a way. I will write two letters. One will be for my grandmother, the valide sultan. You must hide it in the diplomatic post. She will know I am safe and coming home. And then for the ambassador I will write another letter, about this Ahmat – revealing the name of the snake, the turncoat – which you will leave on the ambassador's desk. Only once that is done will I go."

Ezra made up a bed for Loveday in Mrs Boscaven's room. Mahmoud insisted on sleeping on the floor on the top landing, ready for fight or flight. Curled up in a ball, Mahmoud looked less like a sultan, Ezra thought, more like a cat – but Ezra could hardly blame him for his vigilance. Now that Loveday was being hunted too, the threat that surrounded them seemed more real and present than ever.

Before Ezra fell asleep he looked around his empty room and made a small prayer to remember Mr McAdam. Then he blew out his candle stub and prayed for some protection – for Loveday, for Mahmoud and for himself.

The next morning Ezra went out to fetch some breakfast, making sure no one saw him as he left. As he made his way down the street he was wrestling with the problem of how to get inside the Ottoman Embassy unseen. Then he realized he had walked past the St John shop without thinking of Anna once. He turned back. The sign creaked in the breeze. She was in another country, across a sea. Ezra felt a little sad, but that was all. He was glad she wasn't here to see what had happened. She would not approve at all, she would have told him to go to the authorities or forget everything. He would not. The man who shot his master must not walk away. He knew this was the right thing to do. He was certain.

Ezra sped up towards the baker's. His friends would be waiting for breakfast.

When he returned, Loveday had gone, left early, taken her sword. "Mahmoud! You shouldn't have let her go!"

Mahmoud tore off a piece of the loaf Ezra had bought. "You were gone for quite a long time. How could I stop her? She said she had an idea."

Ezra raked his hair with his hands. "She didn't say what she was doing? Where she was going?"

Mahmoud shrugged. "She said not to worry, she had her rapier, and she promised she would be back before dark."

Ezra swore. She would be eyeballing the embassy – she would be seen. She was hardly the sort of girl who faded into the background.

The church bell at St Anne's chimed for nine o'clock. He would give her until twelve, he decided, and then go after her.

All morning Ezra felt as if he were walking on needles. He imagined Loveday thinking she, alone with her sword, could take on the massed Russian cavalry and the combined ranks of the Ottoman Janissary force. Ezra had read about the Janissaries, the Ottoman palace guard, who were, it was said, the fiercest fighting brigade the world over. Or perhaps, Ezra thought, Loveday had gone back to Mr Falcon's lodgings and was going through his things, looking for something that might count as proof of Ahmat's guilt. He remembered how they had first met, Loveday running for her life from a gang of resurrection men. Was she fleeing again now? he thought. Or perhaps it was already over; perhaps they had already put a bullet through her, like the master.

Ezra could not settle, whether to sweep the floor in the kitchen or to read one of the master's books, half of which were still on the shelves, half of which had been packed away in boxes. He took up the post when the postman called and put it on the master's desk, as if in some small compartment of his brain he imagined Mr McAdam coming in from a morning lecture and wanting his letters, neat and tidy, with Mrs Boscaven in the basement brewing coffee, even Toms sulking in the yard.

It was still only eleven. Mahmoud had written his letters and sealed them with the master's wax. He had also, in his most imperious voice, instructed Ezra to discover which was the best jeweller's to which to take the gemstones, and Ezra had promised that as soon as he knew Miss Finch was safe he would see to it. As for the letters, Ezra couldn't imagine how he would even enter the Ottoman Embassy, let alone discover the ambassador's office and his personal post. It was impossible. He would tell Loveday, as soon as she set foot in the house, that it couldn't be done. But then what *could*?

Ezra sighed and piled the post up in date order, the newest at the bottom. He sieved out the ones that were for Dr James McAdam, and the thought of putting them straight onto the fire made him forget Loveday for a moment. The honourable thing would be to re-address them and send them on to Edinburgh, but he reckoned on owing Dr James McAdam barely any honour at all. In fact, if there was to be any accounting of honour, he imagined Dr James's ledger ran into the red for sure. He held the first letter in his hand, wondering if it might even be a crime to open other people's mail. Then he remembered the feeling of walking out of Mr Lashley's lecture, and tore it open.

It was a begging letter from an orphanage concerned with transporting homeless London children to new homes in the north of England, where, it said, *the opportunities for hard work in the new-built cotton mills mean idle hands no longer turn to crime.*

Ezra had heard of children being taken from the streets to work for a pittance a hundred miles away. It did not sound like his idea of charity. He screwed the letter into a ball and threw it into the fireplace for kindling.

He opened another letter, and this one stopped him dead.

It was from Mr Harkaway. He read it twice, three times, then once more. He could scarcely believe it. Mr Harkaway was disputing Dr James's actions. Dr James McAdam had no right, Mr Harkaway had written, to the estate of his uncle, and he should come into the office, the letter said, to be present at the reading of the will. *Though not an executor, Mr McAdam, you are welcome to attend. However, your actions in trying to sell off the museum collection and the estate may be seen as illegal.*

Ezra gave three inner cheers for the unsmiling Mr Harkaway. He kissed the letter, thanked heaven and all its inhabitants and went through the rest of the pile of Dr James's mail like a tornado in a wheatfield.

He discovered the will had not even been read, and although it did not say who the executors were, it gave a date and a time for the reading: four weeks after the master's death. December the first. Only three days away. Ezra whooped with joy and danced round the room. He would not have been forgotten! Dr James was a blackguard and Lashley a fool – as he himself had been – to imagine they had any control over his life. He would swear on his life there would be tools, and perhaps one or two books, that would come to him, and with tools he could do anything. He could set up a small practice – well, perhaps a very small one, above a shop somewhere, in town. It would be a start.

Suddenly he realized Mahmoud was standing in the doorway watching him.

"What," said the boy, his tone at once curious and accusing, "are you doing?"

"Nothing." Ezra straightened up, tucked the letters back in a pile. "A bit of good news, Mahmoud, that's all," he said, feeling a little guilty at his own happiness when Mahmoud's situation was still so uncertain. The first of December – he said the date over and over to himself in case he might forget. But Ezra felt suddenly so lit up with joy he might have hovered a good few inches off the floor.

"That is good for you," Mahmoud said, without much interest. "I have finished my writing and Miss Finch has not returned."

"Ah," Ezra said, and in a moment his joy was swept away by the reminder of Loveday's absence. "Miss Finch – I should see if she is outside the embassy, or perhaps at Mr Falcon's lodgings."

"It has been hours," Mahmoud said. "I would not want any harm to come to Miss Finch."

"Neither would I," Ezra agreed. "I just hope she hasn't started waving that damned blade of hers around and got herself arrested."

It had begun to rain. Ezra took the master's second-best winter coat, which was still on the hook by the front door, snuck out of Ham Yard and turned towards St Martin's Lane. The coat still smelt, comfortingly, of the master's tobacco and snuff. He stuck his hands deep inside the pockets and ran all the way down the slippery mud-spattered streets.

Ezra couldn't remember the number of Mr Falcon's boarding house, but he knew it was next to an inn called the Hogget. He turned his collar up – and ran slap-bang into a young girl clad all in black and in possession of a large carpetbag. The girl let loose a torrent of curses and burnt the air bluer than a summer sky.

Ezra would know those curses anywhere. "Loveday!" It was her, although her hair – well, the hair he could see escaping under her hat – was a deep muddy brown, the colour of the swill that raced down the centre of the street. "It *is* you!"

"Shh!" she hissed. "For heaven's sake, Ezra, I am in disguise. I have a plan. Come on, back to yours, and hurry – I don't want my hair to run. It took all morning and close to a vat of walnut oil pomade to do this!"

"We were worried. You shouldn't have left like that!" Ezra protested as he joined her at a jog. "I thought you were about to attack the Ottomans and the Russians single-handed."

"I am not an idiot, you know," Loveday said, racing on.

Ezra ran to catch up. "You should have told me your plans. You are in danger. They are looking for you!"

She turned around. The rain was cockling the edges of her hat. "They will be looking for a redhead. This is important, Ezra! We need to help Mahmoud, to deliver his letters. And avenge my father and your master – I can think of no worthier or more noble cause for which to dye my hair."

"But Loveday, we tried to get into the embassy, remember? They wouldn't even let us through the door."

"Ah, that is what you think." Now she was smiling. "Mr Falcon was due to play the Ottoman Embassy party, but unfortunately he has passed away. However, this morning, after I dyed my hair, I went to see his agent. The good news is, he has replaced one magic act with another: The Amazing Masked Magician Ezekiel – that's you, by the way – and his Mystic Muse." She bowed. "Me, of course."

Ezra looked at her incredulously as the rain fell down his neck. Mr McAdam's overcoat was too big, and icy raindrops ran down his spine through the gap at the collar, and made him shiver.

"Oh, don't make such a mopish face!" Loveday exclaimed. "I will teach you everything you need to know, and I have taken all the props I need from Mr Falcon's." She held up the bag.

Ezra couldn't say a word.

"You will be fine, more than fine – I am sure you once told me there was a great deal of showmanship involved in being a good surgeon." She began walking again before he could protest, leaving Ezra to watch helplessly as she hurried ahead through the crowds back to Soho.

"Loveday Finch," he said aloud, "what have you done?"

Chapter Fifteen

The Ottoman Embassy
St James's Square
London
November 1792

Ezra had bitten down all of the nails on his right hand. Loveday assured him all would be well – she had drilled them for every waking hour of the past two days, and now Ezra could turn a red handkerchief into a blue one just about passably, and pick the card Mahmoud was thinking of two times out of three, although he suspected Mahmoud was being generous. Whether he could make a young girl vanish into thin air, as he was supposed to do this evening, was quite another matter altogether.

It was just getting dark as he and Loveday neared the embassy building. Mahmoud had been ordered to remain at Great Windmill Street despite his protests, but as the embassy loomed ahead, five storeys high and the width of four regular townhouses at least, Ezra couldn't help feeling that the prince's casual imperiousness might have done their party some good. He shifted the heavy carpetbag of props from one hand to another and hoped that this evening he and Loveday might succeed in their endeavour. What were they after all, he told himself, other than rather extravagant couriers simply delivering post? Then he remembered that Mr Finch had been a courier, and he had ended up dead.

"Come along," Loveday whispered, and Ezra followed her across the square. He wondered what the master would make of this situation – his apprentice about to play a conjuror in front of an audience – then reminded himself that the Ezra McAdam of one month ago would have thought this utterly unbelievable too.

"Are you dreaming?" Loveday said. "Only we have work to do and much of it depends on your wits being as sharp as my blade tonight."

Ezra took a deep breath and pulled on a pair of Mr Falcon's white kid gloves. "I am ready, I promise."

"Now, should anyone ask, you are Ezekiel, and I am Lily." She smiled. "And we will do justice by the dead, help a prince home and uncover a traitor. In the future they will sing songs about us in old Constantinople, I am certain of it!"

Ezra nodded weakly. He wished he could have her confidence. The look on his face must have betrayed his doubts.

"Think of it as a kind of amputation," she said, clapping him on the shoulder. "Only if anything goes wrong it's you and I who are for the chop."

"That didn't help," Ezra retorted as he shifted the heavy bag again and made for the tradesmen's entrance. At least, he thought, it didn't matter much to anyone whether he lived or died; given that, he may as well go down doing the very best he could.

They were shown up to the ballroom on the first floor by a porter – not the same porter as last time, thank heavens, although Loveday had insisted that they would not be recognized with her hair dyed brown. The ballroom ran the length of the palatial building and was fitted out with mirrors and gold leaf. Everything sparkled. Ezra had never seen anything like it – there were candles enough to stock all the chandlers in London.

"Shut your mouth, Ez," Loveday laughed. "You look like a tourist outside St Paul's."

Ezra unpacked their bag. He unfolded and hung up the black velvet backdrop, and Loveday assembled the special table and covered it with a floor-length cloth. At the side of the stage was a tall palm in a pot. Ezra moved it closer.

"There are so many servants," he said, looking around – they were mostly liveried men in cloth-of-gold waistcoats and last season's periwigs. He wondered how many of them still had their tongues. "How on earth can we find out where the ambassador's private office is, let alone get in? What if your gilt doesn't work?"

Loveday patted her pocket. "Mr Falcon swore by it, said it opened every door in the kingdom."

"I think this embassy counts as an outpost of the sultan's."

"You concentrate on your technique," Loveday snapped. "Remember, big arm movements – you're wearing a mask so your body has to do the work for you –" she waved her arms – "like this, sweeping and fluid. And say everything loud and slow and important."

For the first time, Ezra heard a hint of tension in her voice. He nodded.

"We have been over everything many times," he reassured her, laying a hand gently on her arm. He wished he felt as certain as he sounded.

He stood back and looked at their stage. By the time the guests came in it would be darker, and the flickering candlelight might just be enough to hide any flaws in the trick.

A servant led them away to a small dressing room just as the first guests arrived. Ezra walked quickly, trying to hide the side of his face with the scar in case Mr Ahmat was around, but, as Loveday said, it wasn't just his scar that marked him out. Ahmat was unlikely to be fool enough not to recognize him.

"I asked about the ambassador," Loveday told him when they had closed the door on their dressing room. "His office is down the corridor by the front door."

"Are you sure you want to do this, Loveday?" Ezra said. "I mean, we could just slip the letters under the ambassador's door and leave it to good luck?"

"Good luck?" She shook her head. "We are here now. We have to try our best, for Mahmoud. And remember, my name is Lily."

"Lily." Ezra took his mask and hat and left her to change. He pulled the hat down low and made his way back to the ballroom, where he kept himself in the shadows by the side of the stage. A string quartet was playing as the audience came in, high-society London in dresses and coats that would pay Mrs Boscaven's wages for a whole year. Ezra had never seen so many of the well-to-do in one place in all his life – no wonder, he thought, they had not been able to gain entry simply by asking.

Most of the talk was in diplomat's French, and Ezra could only understand snatches of it – mostly trivia concerning horses or cards.

Ezra caught sight of the man he presumed was the ambassador wearing a turban higher than all the other turbans in the room, with a red crown and a sort of billowing white rim that framed his face. He wore a floor-length robe not dissimilar to the one Ezra had seen hanging on the back of Mr Finch's door, brightly coloured in rich reds and blues, and shining in the candlelight. He was talking to some elderly bewigged English men when someone caught his sleeve and whispered something in his ear, a thin man, wearing a strange combination of European and Turkish dress, a turban with a high-collared, close-fitting frock-coat. Ezra recognized him straight away, and it was like a blow to the chest.

Mr Ahmat, his master's murderer.

It was him, the very man Ezra had last seen in the museum at Great Windmill Street when he had just shot the master. Ezra wished he had Loveday's rapier; he pictured himself crossing the ballroom floor and pinning him to the wall. Making him confess, making him tell the whole room what he had done – two men dead and another hung because of him, and two more poisoned – five deaths in all. And yet Ahmat was more ordinary-looking than Ezra remembered. He might have been oddly dressed, but his face was composed, even personable, his small greying beard neatly trimmed. Ezra would never have guessed this was a man who could shoot another in cold blood. How could you be responsible for so much evil and look as if none of it touched you? Ezra thought. He could feel himself shaking with anger at the injustice of it all. He took slow, deep breaths, trying to compose himself. He must put the loathsome man out of his mind, as much as that was possible. He could not let himself be undone by him, not now.

"I saw him," Ezra said. "The murderer." He was back in the dressing room, where Loveday had transformed herself, with the aid of Mr McAdam's best bed linen, into something she said approximated a Delphic Oracle – albeit a Delphic Oracle with a rapier in the folds of her toga.

"You are sure he didn't see you?" Loveday asked.

Ezra shook his head and put on his mask. It was hot and he could only see the world in two small, round portholes.

Loveday took his hand and squeezed it and they walked into the ballroom together and climbed up on the stage.

"Slowly, calmly," she whispered.

Ezra squeezed her hand in return then turned and faced the crowd, and swallowed hard. There were so many of them, all looking expectantly at him. He shut his eyes and remembered the master at that last lecture at Bart's. The way he had caught everyone's eye, the way he spoke, commanding and direct and confident.

Ezra let go of Loveday's hand; he scanned the audience from one side of the hall to the other. "Gentlemen!" he said, and the crowd quietened. He had their attention. So far, so good. At the edge of his vision he could see Loveday throwing wild shapes, cutting the air with her rapier.

Ezra turned the red handkerchief blue and then back to red as if it were nothing. "Ladies! Behold, the wonders of the universe will now be revealed! Before your very eyes I will make this beautiful young lady –" they were hanging on his words – "vanish!"

There was a ripple of applause. Inside the mask he felt a trickle of sweat roll down his face.

"Lily, the table." He took her hand and she climbed up onto the table.

"Your blade!" She threw the rapier down to Ezra and he caught it in his gloved hand – it nicked the fabric, and the crowd were lucky not to catch him wincing. If the gloves had not been kid, she would have drawn blood.

Loveday stood quite still on the table, her face icy pale as if she truly imagined her own end was close. She was a good actress.

Ezra swished the blade. His near miss had given him an idea.

During anatomy lectures students often pleaded regret and surprise at the lack of blood; blood always got the most attention, the best response. He remembered Mr Lashley once nicking the femoral artery and causing a veritable fountain of the stuff.

Ezra paused, took the rapier in his right hand, held up his left. He passed the blade between the fore and middle fingers, cutting through the kid and into his own flesh. It stung a short sharp pain, but he continued to hold up his left hand so the crowd could watch as the glove, once white, stained red. They gasped. "Ladies and gentlemen, my blade is true!"

Ezra smiled behind his mask. He felt his confidence

growing. Perhaps he enjoyed taking risks more than he imagined.

Loveday twitched; she hadn't expected it either. Good, Ezra thought.

While they were still surprised, he cut the ribbon that held up the curtain, and a month's salary's worth of black silk velvet dropped down in front of Loveday. Ezra realized he was shaking and gripped the sword more tightly. The trick would work, he told himself. They would not be discovered. They would not be set upon by armed guards. They would not be killed.

Not yet.

Ezra pointed the rapier out into the crowd. He would have liked to linger on Mr Ahmat for a few seconds longer, but instead he whirled round and slashed the fabric into ribbons. This was actually most satisfying, and the blade was so sharp the velvet rained down like soft black soot.

Loveday was gone. The crowd didn't quite burst into applause and Ezra knew what they were thinking: she was under the table. He lifted the cloth with the blade, slowly, just slow enough to give her time to vanish through a slit in the backdrop, shed her toga, tie an old white apron of Ellen's over her black mourning dress and break into the ambassador's office.

Ezra lifted the tablecloth higher, higher, then switched it off completely. She had gone. He was alone on the stage.

The crowd applauded. Ezra bowed low. His hand hurt, but he had enjoyed it. Now he felt the mask slipping, though, and he had to leave the stage crabwise to avoid it falling off completely.

The string quartet was setting up again, and struck up a tune Ezra recognized, by Mozart. He resisted the urge to remove the mask, bundled up Loveday's toga and headed back to the dressing room. But in his haste he found himself in a corridor that he'd never seen before, lined with doors.

He couldn't think which way he'd come. He dropped the mask just as a man came out of the room nearest to him. Ezra was scrabbling around on the floor when he came close, and he could see from the man's brown leather slippers, backless in the Ottoman style, that he was a servant.

Ezra stood up and smiled at him. "Excuse me. I am lost, I'm afraid. I was looking for the dressing room?"

The man looked at him blankly.

"I am the magician," Ezra said. "Magician?" He put down Loveday's toga and the mask and turned the red handkerchief blue. The man smiled but made no sound.

"Conjuror?" Ezra spoke slowly.

The man opened his mouth. He had no tongue. Ezra tried not to look unsettled.

"Don't worry, I'll find it. Thank you." Ezra picked up his things and shuffled back the way he had come as quickly as he could.

He turned another corner, mask in hand, when he saw two more men, walking towards him from the other end of the corridor. One was another servant, dressed in the same Turkish livery. The other, severe in his dark frock-coat, was Ahmat. His master's killer. Ezra jammed on his mask and ducked into a doorway, his heart hammering louder than hoofbeats on stone.

Ahmat was talking, not with words but with the Ixarette, the sign language Mahmoud had told him about. They were coming this way; they would pass him in an instant. Why were they here – surely the function was not over yet – and what were they saying? Was Loveday discovered? Had she found her way into the office, or had she been seen? Was Ahmat sounding the silent alarm among the servants right now, a warning that some girl was breaking into the ambassador's office? Then surely it was better if Ahmat was here, dealing with him, Ezra thought. He could buy Loveday some precious time. He took off his mask and stepped into the light so he could be seen.

"Mr Ahmat," Ezra declared bravely, his hand on Loveday's blade. "An amazing recovery for a man hung for murder."

Ahmat clapped his hands and the servant ran away down the corridor, not once looking back.

"Who are you?" The man's face was sour. He looked Ezra up and down. "Ah, I know! The McAdam boy. I see. Perhaps you think you are doing your dead master some kind of service by threatening me? I'm afraid you'll find Mr Ahmat is dead. That is not my name." He bowed a little. "I also think you are very stupid in your choice of weapon. I long ago exchanged the blade for the gun. So much cleaner and more modern, don't you think?"

Ezra was sure Ahmat couldn't have a gun on him, the coat was too close. He took a step forward, sword out. The man backed away. Ezra felt suddenly stronger, braver, than ever before – he'd never in his life been anywhere near a fight, but the same spirit he'd felt on stage seemed to course through his body. He felt as if he could do anything. He pressed the tip of the blade against Ahmat's collarbone. The man did not flinch.

Anger flared up inside Ezra. "You have killed my master," he said fiercely, "and countless others. You would betray your own countrymen…"

Mr Ahmat moved the blade away from his neck with one hand, and with the other opened the door behind him.

"As I remarked, a stupid boy," he said, and stepped back into a stateroom where a vast portrait of a man whom Ezra presumed was the sultan hung over the fireplace.

Ezra threw down the toga and the mask and strode after him.

"I know you are plotting with the Russians. I have seen you with him, with Oleg. You want a war, your own country overthrown."

"You over-dramatize. I would simply rather a sultan of my choosing, a sultan who kept his place," Ahmat replied, still backing away. "And if the Russians can help us achieve that, then so be it."

"I will tell!" Ezra cried. "I will tell the ambassador you are in league with your empire's enemies. I will tell the sultan himself!"

The man gave a thin laugh. "How do you propose that feat, young man? Magic? And who would believe a dead surgeon's slave?" As he spoke he felt along the massive wooden table for a drawer and pulled.

"I am not a slave!" Ezra leapt forward onto the table and almost slipped on the polished surface. He righted himself just as Ahmat tried another drawer – Ezra could see he was having trouble, but there might be a gun in there, or another weapon. Ezra did not want to die. It was kill or be killed.

He jabbed the blade down across the man's chest, but Ahmat stood firm. "Do you expect me to crumple? To lie down and give up? You are used to dead bodies, I think, and they are not known for fighting back."

Ezra turned the sword handle over in his hand. The man was right. He was sweating, even in the fireless room. Ahmat leant forward, grinning.

"You have not the stomach for it, do you? You can carve the meat but you can't kill the sheep."

Ezra gripped the blade tighter and drew back, ready to lunge downwards and into the man's heart. He had sliced flesh so many times in his life, uncovered ribcages, sawn off the top of skulls. Eviscerated boys and girls, men and women. But a living man, a living, breathing man, even one as worthless as this, who had killed his master, who would cause more death and heartbreak if left alive – he could not do it. He wiped the sweat from his face, and in that moment, Ahmat picked up a glass paperweight from the table and slammed it hard against Ezra's shin. The pain exploded in his leg and he lost his balance and fell sideways off the table, blade still tight in his hand.

Ahmat pulled open yet another drawer and took out a gun, which he pointed straight at Ezra.

Though the pain in Ezra's leg was great, he stared back at Ahmat as the gunman squeezed the trigger – he would not die a coward.

There was a click. Ahmat squeezed again, another click. Ezra felt a wash of relief, and as Ahmat scrabbled in the drawer for bullets and began to load the gun, Ezra dragged himself upright – he had to get out, to find Loveday and run.

Ezra hauled himself into the corridor and slammed the door shut behind him. He ran towards the servants' staircase as fast as he could. His shin felt as if it were on fire.

"Loveday!" He leant over the banister and shouted into the stairwell as loud as he could. "Loveday!"

Three faces peered up, two servants and one very cross, brown-haired girl.

"My name," she hissed back from the floor below, "is Lily! Where have you been?"

"He's after me. We have to get out."

Loveday picked up her skirts and ran up to him.

"He's behind me, with a gun," Ezra whispered urgently. Loveday frowned when she saw he was limping, but there was no time for questions.

"Up. This way," she said, "and I'll have that back." She took the rapier and pulled him along behind her, taking the stairs two at a time.

They heard the door to the staircase push open and Ahmat yelling in what Ezra took to be Turkish. He fired the gun and they pressed themselves into the wall.

"Keep going!" Loveday cried. "The way downstairs is blocked – there are too many people. We have to find another way down."

The top floor was a maze of servants' bedrooms, empty for the most part, and Loveday tore through, looking for a way out. Ezra rested, leaning against the metal frame of a bed in one of the rooms, breathing deeply; he pulled back his stocking and saw a huge yellow-black bruise against the bone. Then he realized he was being watched. A small boy, dressed in full Turkish livery. Some kind of page, no doubt.

From the foot of the stairs they could hear Ahmat yelling. "Someone is after you?" the boy said. His English was strongly accented. "Are you bandits?"

"No," Loveday cried, appearing at Ezra's side. "He," she pointed at Ezra with her rapier, "is Truth and I am Beauty and we are being threatened by the devil himself."

The boy gasped. More voices came from the stairs. "Ali Pasha, the devil..."

Ezra crouched down to the boy's level. "We need help. Please? Which way?"

Loveday tried a door, but it only led through to another room. She swished her blade in irritation and the boy backed into the adjoining room, afraid of the sword.

"It's all right," Ezra said. "She won't hurt you. But the man behind us..."

They could hear the thundering of footsteps coming up towards the attics.

"Come on!" Loveday said impatiently, pulling Ezra away from the door.

"No – this way is better." The boy nodded them inside and opened the bedroom window. It led directly out onto the roof.

"Of course!" Loveday wedged a chair under the door handle and climbed outside. The night seemed cold and dark and cloudy as soot.

"There is a clear run across the roof," the boy said. "You can get down to the park if you go quickly. We take the small ones to see the pelicans sometimes."

"Thank you," Ezra said to the boy. Someone had begun banging on the door. "Thank you!" He looked out; he could just make out Loveday standing in the valley between the pitched roofs. He swallowed. At least, he told himself, the darkness was such that he couldn't see where the roof ended and the night began.

"Now where?" Loveday shouted, the wind whipping her voice away.

The thumping on the bedroom door was as loud as cannon.

"I can show you!" The boy squeezed out after Ezra just as the bedroom door flew open.

"Stop!" Ahmat yelled. Ezra thought he could hear others with him, and imagined those Turkish guards with their heavy curved swords.

"Get down!" Loveday shouted. Ahmat fired out of the window after them into the dark, once, twice, three times. Ezra heard one bullet whistle past his head, another slam into slate, shattering tiles, then he heard the boy gasp, as though surprised, and felt him fall against him, shuddering as the life left his body.

Ezra cursed. If only he'd had the guts to kill the man when he had the chance.

"You're a murderer!" he yelled. "You've betrayed your whole country! Do you hear me?" He stood up, leaning against the roof and shouting into the wind. Another bullet whirred past and cannoned into the roof tiles.

"Ezra," Loveday hissed, "for heaven's sake, let's try and leave with our lives. Look, he's reloading. Come on."

Ezra checked for the boy's pulse, then when he was

sure there was none, he laid the page boy's head down gently.

"Come on!"

As the pair reached the end of the valley they heard Ahmat step out after them.

"I think we're trapped," Loveday hissed into the darkness.

"We can't be! There has to be a way down. The boy said…"

"Do you see one?" Loveday was angry again. "I can't see a damn thing!"

"Well, if we can't, then neither can he," Ezra whispered. "I have an idea. Give me your blade."

"Don't be an idiot," Loveday whispered back, handing it over.

Ezra shimmied up the side of the valley roof. He didn't really have an idea; his only thought was to finish what he should have done earlier and hope that Loveday would get away if he did not. If he could only get behind or above the man somehow.

"I can hear you," Mr Ahmat said.

His voice was cold and hard as ice. The man would kill without a thought. They were both as good as dead.

"You are cornered. There is no way down – although you could save me some ammunition and dash your brains out."

Ezra felt the wind whip past him. He did not want to die; he would not die, not at the hands of this monster. He felt the anger boiling up inside and picked up a roof tile and threw it in the direction of Ahmat's voice. He heard it break and shatter. He threw another and another, then Loveday started the same thing until the night was filled with the sound of slates breaking.

"You cannot kill me with roof tiles," said Ahmat scornfully.

Ezra slid down towards the man's voice, saw his shadow against the charcoal sky, and slashed with the blade. Then he saw the flash from the gun as it fired – he smelt the gunpowder before he felt the burning as the pellet drove into his shoulder and forced his arm out and back. The pain was intense. He lost his grip on Loveday's rapier and dropped to his knees.

Then he was aware of a flurry of black cloth and some kind of scuffle. There was the sound of a blade slicing flesh and Ezra saw someone stagger back – the gun went off again, a bright orange flash and a loud crack, and then the sound of someone falling, slumping down.

"Loveday? Loveday!"

"I think," came her voice out of the darkness, a little out of breath, "the man is dead."

Mr Ahmat lay on his back, his hands both at his neck, the blood still frothing around his splayed fingers. She had killed him, sliced him ear to ear.

"Am I dying?" Ezra said.

Loveday wiped the blood off her sword and cut his shirt away from his shoulder, and began to laugh. She put her face close to his. "A flesh wound! You are no more going to die than I am the Emperor of China. Come on, Ezra, get up. We have to go home."

"But you killed him, Loveday. You killed a man!"

"For heaven's sake, Ez. How can I have killed a man who was already hanged and dead, close to a week ago?"

Chapter Sixteen

The McAdam Memorial Anatomical Lecture Theatre
Great Windmill Street
Soho
London
1 March 1793

"Gentlemen! Your watches, please!" Ezra looked round the room at the expectant, anxious faces gathered there. The theatre was packed. Ezra made sure to look into the eyes of each and every one of those present, or at least as many as he could, before he set the timer on his pocket watch. Well, he called it his watch, but he always thought of it as the master's.

"I begin!" he said. "Flesh knife, Jos." Josiah passed him the flesh knife. Ezra had paid to buy him out of the army, and was sure he'd have found no better assistant in the whole city.

The man on the table screamed as Ezra cut away the stinking, gangrenous flesh around his forearm. There was not enough skin to make a flap, but he had done this before, he could improvise; he would just have to cut the bone slightly higher up.

"Bone saw!"

This time there were no mistakes. The operation may have taken a good thirty seconds longer than the master's record, but Ezra was happy.

"Good job, Ez," Jos said. "Your master'd be best pleased."

"Yes." Ezra smiled. "I do believe he would."

They both admired the bandaged stump. Its owner, a boatman who'd been crushed by falling barrels, said nothing; he had passed out a good three minutes ago with the sound of metal on bone.

Ezra accepted the congratulations of various students, untied his apron and went back into the house. He had to pinch himself, his life could not be in any way more perfect than it was right now. In fact it could only have been better if the master had still been alive – the house was not the same without him, and Ezra often found himself wishing he could have asked Mr McAdam for his advice or assistance. But he had a fine library, and down in the kitchen he could smell the coffee Mrs Boscaven was brewing up. Ezra went into his office and began to deal with the post.

He sat down at his desk and sighed. Last winter seemed to belong in a different century – Loveday Finch and Mahmoud, fifth son of the Ottoman sultan, eating a picnic of hot pies on the floor. Performing magic at the Ottoman Embassy, and escaping – narrowly – with their lives.

They were lucky that the ambassador had faith in Mahmoud's assertion that Izmet Ali Pasha – the man Ezra knew as Ahmat – had indeed been in league with the Russians. And the fact that he had killed one of his page boys counted against him too, of course.

Loveday and Ezra had been allowed to leave – surely, Ezra had told her, the only girl to have admitted killing a man and to have walked free. Loveday said she had every right to do so; after all, she was, at the very least, avenging her father and her father's friend, and Ezra's master to boot. And anyway, she said, it was a fact that Mr Izmet Ali Pasha, under a different name, had already been sentenced to hang, so all she had done was carry out the letter of the king's law.

Loveday and Mahmoud had left London soon after the incident at the embassy, with two of the Cherries of Edirne exchanged for cash, and taken a stagecoach to Dover. Although Mahmoud had insisted that he could travel across Europe quite safely alone, Loveday had said she would escort him back to Constantinople. Ezra agreed that Loveday made the best sort of bodyguard.

The will had been like some kind of blessing. A complete and utter reversal of fortune. Dr James's actions had been illegal. The house was not for sale: it had been left, title deeds and all, to Ezra McAdam, free man of property – along with the chance to complete his apprenticeship with occasional lessons from Mr Gordon at the Middlesex hospital. The museum had been gifted to the College of Surgeons with Ezra as a nominated curator, able to arrange and take care of the exhibits just as he had done in the past.

Ezra could never have imagined a better outcome. The fire was roaring as he slipped off his boots and rested his stockinged feet against the guard. There was a long letter from Monsieur Bichat – a continuation of a discussion they'd been having in letters since the New Year. His thesis was that the brain could exist independently of the body. He should know: the guillotine was very busy in Paris at the moment, Monsieur Bichat wrote, and they had a bounty of decapitations to experiment on. One of his colleagues swore he had seen a head speak, seconds after being parted from its body. Ezra almost laughed as he finished reading.

There were a couple of other letters, but they looked uninteresting. One small square of paper, however, did catch his eye. He knew that curved hand.

He looked up at the calendar. It was over two months since they'd left. According to the journey they had mapped out together, the pair should be in Italy by now, at least, catching a boat from Naples or Genoa east across the Mediterranean and, given a good crossing, back to Constantinople by April.

He tore the letter open. It was dated January the twentieth, why had it taken so long to reach him?

20th January 1793

Dear Ezra,

Bad news, the worst. I have lost Mahmoud in Paris. The Russian was in the city already and by now the dye has washed out of my hair. We were trying to get a coach south out of the city but it is hell; the mob is on the street and nothing – nowhere – is safe.

I am sorry to write to you but there is no one else. I go out every day and scour the streets for him but am worried it may be too late.

Your friend,
Loveday

Ezra put the letter down. He pushed his feet back into his shoes and stood up.

"Mrs B!" he called down to the kitchen. "I am going away. I think I shall be a couple of weeks."

Acknowledgements

Books are a bit like children in that it takes so many people to actually help them into the world. The people below are my book midwives – and thanks to all of you for a smooth and stitch-free delivery.

A huge thank you to everyone at Walker. I had always wanted to be published by Walker because they have lovely books and a lovely building, and I have not been disappointed. Thanks to the design team, Jack and Royston, for my best cover ever, and to Emma for being fantastic – what would books do without editors!

I also have to thank my daughter, Harry. I know she gets a dedication but she loved the story right away and every day after I'd finished writing she would check it over and query some of the more ridiculous stuff I'd come up with and make it better. She'd supply answers when I got stuck, and this would be a much poorer book without her.

Also friends and fellow authors for listening to moans (see, it is like childbirth!) and finally Stephanie, my long-suffering agent and Fritz, my even longer-suffering boyfriend, partner and husband.

Catherine Johnson is an award-winning writer of Welsh/African Caribbean descent, now living in Hastings in East Sussex. Her novels for children include *Stella*; *The Dying Game*; *Arctic Hero*, which was selected for Booked Up; *A Nest of Vipers*, which was shortlisted for the UKLA Award; and *The Curious Tale of the Lady Caraboo*, shortlisted for the YA Book Prize and nominated for the Carnegie Medal.

Of the inspiration for *Sawbones*, Catherine says, "This book initially grew very, very quickly. A couple of years ago when my grown-up son was still living at home we would go on trips to places we'd never been. My daughter recommended the Hunterian Museum in Lincoln's Inn Fields. If you have never been and have a strong stomach, go! It is brilliant. John Hunter was a pioneering surgeon and anatomist who lived in Soho at the end of the eighteenth century. He loved dissection and his collection holds lots of macabre but interesting stuff, including a tumour that had been removed from a boy's face, and that was what started me off with Ezra. What if a surgeon like Hunter had taken the boy as a subject – a slave, perhaps – bought him as an oddity, removed the tumour and trained him up? I wrote the first draft faster than I had written any book in my life!"

Sawbones went on to win the Young Quills Award for Historical Fiction and Catherine has now written a sequel, *Blade and Bone*. She also writes for film and TV, including *Holby City*, and her radio play *Fresh Berries* was nominated for the Prix d'Italia. She works regularly with children and teachers in primary schools and libraries across the UK. To find out more about Catherine and her writing, go to:

www.catherinejohnson.co.uk